BACHE

Perry's marriage to Nash Devereux had been a 'paper' one—just for convenience—and she hadn't seen him for years. Now she wanted to marry Trevor Coleman; so, for a start, she must get the marriage annulled. But why on earth did Nash then announce that he was hoping for a reconciliation?

BACHELOR'S WIFE

BY

JESSICA STEELE

MILLS & BOON LIMITED
15–16 BROOK'S MEWS
LONDON W1A 1DR

First published 1981
Australian copyright 1981
Philippine copyright 1981
This edition 1981

© Jessica Steele 1981

ISBN 0 263 73534 6

Set in Monophoto Baskerville 10 on 11 pt.

Made and printed in Great Britain by
Richard Clay (The Chaucer Press) Ltd,
Bungay, Suffolk

CHAPTER ONE

'I'M going to have to do something about you, Perry.'

The disappointed ardour as Trevor's arms fell away was not missed by her. Nor the admission that he was no longer prepared to put up with the way she allowed their lovemaking to go so far but no farther.

'I'm sorry.' The apology came automatically. It was easier than trying to explain what she didn't fully understand herself, that returning his love as she did, she found it impossible to go past that barrier. But she loved him, and didn't want to part bad friends. 'Will you come in for coffee?'

'Is there any point?'

Stifling a sigh, Perry reached for the car door handle. Trevor, for all he was a dear most of the time, was inclined to sulk if things didn't go his way.

'Perhaps not,' she answered, a shade more sharply than she meant, but something inside her not liking that he was putting her in the wrong. Then her voice softened, fear catching her that he might have grown too fed up to want to see her again. 'Goodnight, Trevor. Thank you . . .'

His hand stayed her before she could leave the car. 'I'll give you a ring tomorrow,' he said, much to her relief. 'I don't suppose you'll change your mind and come with me to visit Mother tomorrow night, will you?'

Because he seemed to have quickly got over his sulks and was once again the Trevor she loved, Perry almost said yes, she would go with him.

'I promised Mrs Foster I'd give her a hand with a dress she's making tomorrow,' she suddenly remembered, truthfully.

'Why you bother with that old woman beats me,' he replied, letting her know he wasn't so completely over his sulks as she had thought and was ready to be offended at the smallest suggestion that she preferred someone else's company to his. 'I know she's your landlady, but . . .'

'That has nothing to do with it.' Perry could feel herself beginning to get annoyed at his suggestion that she was keeping in with her landlady for her own ends. 'I like her, and besides . . .' She stopped, realising it wouldn't be very tactful to say, 'Besides, you always see your mother on a Tuesday evening, so I felt free to make my own arrangements.'

'Besides which,' he put in, 'you can't stand my mother.'

'It's not that.' It was a lie.

Perry had no difficulty in recalling the cold atmosphere of Mrs Coleman's house, the continual carping of the woman, conversation always coming interminably round to the same worn-out subject of divorce. How Trevor's father had left her when he was small to go off and live with his fancy woman. Trevor was a grown man now, but the years had not softened the hatred Mrs Coleman felt for her ex-husband. It was a constant thorn in her side that, although she was determined never to divorce him, with a change in the divorce laws, he had turned round and divorced her. Perry had heard chapter and verse of what Mrs Coleman thought on the iniquity of divorce.

'Can't say I really blame you,' Trevor said suddenly, putting an arm round her and pulling her closer, ignoring her lie as if she hadn't uttered it. 'Mother's a bit of a pain, isn't she?' And before she could reply, though she had no idea what she could say to that, Trevor had returned to being the wonderful person she had some months ago started to think of him as being. 'I don't want to go myself,' he confessed, 'but if I don't Mother will be on that phone at the first opportunity giving me what for.'

Knowing she could never have spoken of her mother the way he had spoken of his, had she been lucky enough to still have her, Perry stayed quiet, happy to have his arm around her, his sulks a thing of the past.

'I've grown up having the evils of divorce stuffed down my throat,' he said, his lips brushing her honey-gold hair. 'That's why it's so important to me to be sure. I need to be sure that you and I are right before . . .'

He broke off to begin a passionate onslaught on her mouth. But for the first time Perry wasn't giving her full attention to his amorous intent. Her heart turned over at what he had just said. Did he mean what she wanted him to mean? That he wanted to be sure before he asked her to marry him?

Her heartbeats hurried, but she wasn't at all certain if her fast beating heart was from what he had said or from the sudden feeling of panic his words aroused. She wanted to marry him, yes, yes, she did, but . . .

Realising she wasn't participating as fully as she had on other occasions, Trevor drew back. 'What's wrong?' The enquiry came with a hint of temper.

'What—what did you mean just now, about . . .'

'About us?' Temper went from him. She could hear a smile in his voice as he said, 'Oh, come on, Perry, surely you knew?'

She found difficulty in answering, her mind in too much of a whirl with the complications she saw in front of her if it really was marriage Trevor had in mind.

'You said something about being sure before . . .'

He took his arms from her, leaving her feeling cold—and worried. He turned to face the front, and with his eyes staring at the windscreen at last brought out, in almost a detached way, she thought, her mind in uproar:

'I hadn't meant to say anything yet. But since we've got this far, since you already know how I feel about you, have told me you love me, then I might as well tell you I've been thinking along the lines of asking you to marry me.'

'Oh,' said Perry, a mixture of emotions rioting through

her, her love for him uppermost, her wish, for all it didn't sound as though he was actually proposing, to be his wife. And at the same time that other emotion, fear. Fear to tell him in case he wouldn't understand. Wouldn't understand and would say goodbye to her for ever.

'That I haven't put that particular question yet is because of my parents.'

'Your parents?' Confusion was added. What did his parents have to do with him asking her to marry him? His mother she didn't like, but she was sensitive enough to know he must be fond of her. And without parents herself, she would want that he gave his parents all the consideration due. But . . .

'My parents' marriage was a disaster,' he stated. 'You've heard my mother riding her favourite hobbyhorse, you know her strong views against divorce. Views I'm bound to say that have been handed down to me.'

Perry's vocal chords felt strangled. 'You mean,' she asked chokily, panic with her that even if she did have the nerve to tell him that secret locked up inside her, it would be the end, 'you mean you share her strong feelings against divorce?'

'It's all right for other people,' he declared, and to her keenly pitched ears sounding a touch pompous as he said it, 'but it would never do for me. Once married, I intend to stay married.'

'I see,' she murmured, at a loss to find anything smarter to put in.

'So you see, Perry, I have to be very sure before I commit myself.'

Her head was spinning when five minutes later she let herself into her flat. She should have told him, she thought, annoyed with herself for letting the opportunity go by. They were already discussing divorce, the time was so right to tell him.

Coward, coward, she called herself as she undressed ready for bed. The time had been so right, she told herself

again as she seated herself before her dressing table mirror
and brushed her shoulder-length silky hair. She met wide
green eyes in the mirror and saw without interest her perfect features and clear, almost translucent skin. Oh, why
hadn't she told him? It would all have been over with
now. He had said divorce was all right for other people.
He would have understood, she knew he would. Why, he
had said that night he had told her he loved her that it
was her loyalty he found her most endearing quality!

Though that loyalty had annoyed him a time or two
when occasionally he had called unexpectedly to pick her
up from work and found her working late in order to
finish off a dress or some other item wanted urgently.

But he would have understood about her loyalty to
Ralph, though to her mind it had been more love for her
stepfather that had made her do what she had to help him
out of that awful mess he was in.

Still regretting that she had hoarded her guilty secret to
her like some miser, Perry put down her hairbrush and
chewed her thumbnail for several moments until her eyes
fastened on the jewel box that had belonged to her
mother.

The jewel box housed very little that was of any value.
She pulled it towards her as though compelled, lifting the
lid and putting aside the top compartment that held a few
items of inexpensive jewellery. And there at the bottom
she saw it—the evidence, for all it was a copy. A copy sent
for after Ralph had died when everything then seemed to
be too incredible to be true, confirmation needed that
what had happened really had happened.

Her hands shaking revealing the agitation she was in,
she picked up the piece of rolled paper and spread it out.
She read it as she had read it before—it said it all. Perry
Bethia Grainger, seamstress, aged eighteen, had six
years ago married one Nash Devereux, engineer, aged
thirty.

She rolled the copy of her marriage certificate up again

and replaced it in her jewel box. Trevor would understand when she told him why she had done it—wouldn't he?

Surprised that when she had eventually got off to sleep she had slept quite well, Perry had her usual scramble round the next morning. She always liked to be on time at work, for all old Mr Ratcliffe never turned a hair on the few occasions she didn't make it.

'How's my best tailor?' he greeted her as she went in.

'You'd better keep your voice down or you'll have Madge walking out on you,' she replied, giving him a cheerful grin.

'Then don't tell her,' he said, his white head bobbing as he reeled back in mock horror.

She entered the workroom where Madge already had her head down. 'Morning, Madge,' she greeted, as her friend and colleague looked up.

'Morning.' Madge, somewhere in the region of forty-five, was a joy to work with. 'Put the kettle on, there's a dear. I've come in early because I want to go early and didn't have time for coffee before I left home. Don't forget to tell old Ratty that when he sees me sloping off before he blows his five o'clock hooter.'

Perry laughed. It was impossible to be down for long in Madge's company. But she couldn't stop the thoughts she had had last night from returning to torment her.

She could understand Trevor with his background wanting to be sure before he asked her to marry him. Yet if he did ask her, and her eyes glowed at the thought of being his wife, then she would have to tell him.

Yes, definitely she would have to tell him. But, prompted something inside her, wouldn't it be better to tell him *after* the marriage had been annulled rather than before?

She grew excited at the idea, calling herself all sorts of a fool for having wasted all these years in not doing some-thing about it before this. She couldn't think why she hadn't. She should have realised the possibility that some time she was likely to want to get married, a real marriage this time.

What was it that had made her keep putting it off? Admittedly it had crossed her mind several times that she ought to do something about it. Was it that not liking Nash Devereux, having found him a particularly cold, charmless person, she had hoped that he might be the one to instigate the divorce?

She remembered his hard eyes, the way he had told her in no uncertain terms the way he felt about women, and saw then that she should have known he wouldn't be the one instigate divorce proceedings. Unless his views on women had changed mightily, then he had every intention of staying a married bachelor.

Oh, he liked women well enough for everything but marriage; there had been ample evidence of that over the years. Wealthy, well known in the business world, having come a long way since he had referred to the giant concern it now was as simply 'the Works', he was forever being reported in the papers. He had been well off six years ago, Perry remembered, but even so he must have worked night and day to make the Devereux Corporation what it was. Though if those pictures of him in the papers, invariably with some beautiful female hanging on to him, rarely the same girl twice, were anything to go by then he still found plenty of time to play.

Aware that she was on the verge of being bitter, she realised she had absolutely no cause. Nash had kept his side of the bargain just as she had kept hers. There was no earthly reason why she should get uptight about him. They should be able to meet, if not as friends, then at least without animosity.

And meet they would have to, she decided, the idea of doing something about getting her marriage to Nash Devereux annulled suddenly cementing. Or if they didn't actually meet, some contact at least had to be made so the wheels could be put in motion to get their marriage ended.

Perry began to feel better, seeing in her mind's eye Trevor eventually proposing. Of her confessing her secret, being able to show him her decree absolute or whatever it was called. Suddenly she glanced up and saw Madge looking at her.

'You've been looking as though you had the world on your shoulders,' Madge remarked. 'Anything wrong?'

'Nothing a quick phone call won't cure,' she answered lightly, hoping it would be that easy. 'If you want to leave early I'll give you a hand, but first I must make my call.'

'If it's private you'd do better to go to the phone box at the end of the street,' Madge opined; there was nowhere private in the old-fashioned building that housed cutters, machinists, pressers, and sundry other staff, not to mention the telephonist who regularly monitored the calls.

Mr Ratcliffe came in just as Perry had picked up her bag. 'I'll be five minutes,' she said by way of excuse for going out.

'Take ten,' he said, his brand of sarcasm amusing her. She knew he didn't mean it.

'Teacher's pet,' came from Madge.

'Jealous,' said Mr Ratcliffe as she went out. Perry smiled; she knew they liked one another and would keep up a verbal sparring for the five minutes she would be out.

Once out in the March wind she forgot about them. She barely noticed the wind that frolicked in her hair, her mind then was only on what she had to say to Nash Devereux. Had he not been such a well-known figure there would be no need to contact him. She could more easily have filed for one of those quickie divorces she had heard about.

But with his every action reported in the press, or so it seemed, she couldn't risk the publicity. Publicity wasn't something she courted. She would hate it even if there wasn't Trevor to think of. Her breath caught as she had terrifying visions of the press somehow getting hold of Trevor's name and she knew then that it was essential that her divorce was kept quiet. Trevor would be horrified to see himself in print as 'the other man'; it would be an end to any plans he had for them. Her imagination went further as she saw in her mind's eye Trevor's mother, absolutely horrified, throwing a fit at the merest suggestion that her son might dare consider marrying a divorcee. Her name would be mud—Mrs Coleman would turn Trevor against her, she knew it. She would keep on and on at him until . . .

Quickly she entered the telephone kiosk, a sick feeling inside of her as she hunted up the number of the Devereux Corporation.

With nervous fingers she dialled, urging herself to remember as the number rang that she had far more confidence now than she had possessed at eighteen. It would no longer be like it was six years ago when Nash's air of sophistication, that terrible cold way he had had with her, had frightened the thin, gawky girl she had been. She was twenty-four now, for goodness' sake, with most of her uncertain edges smoothed away. She was still slender, but had curved out in the right places. And what with her skill as a needlewoman she had a wardrobe that was smart and modern. She even possessed some clothes that could make her look as sophisticated as any of the females she had seen photographed with the man who in a very few moments she would be speaking with.

'Devereux Corporation.'

The voice was clear, just the right hint of warmth, a splendid advert for the big conglomerate that went under the Devereux name.

'Mr Devereux, please.' She was glad to hear that confident note there. That it was in direct contrast to the way her insides were behaving the telephonist would never know.

'Mr Devereux is not available. Can anyone else help you?'

Perhaps she had been expecting too much to be put straight through to him, Perry thought.

'No,' she said, her voice still managing to sound confident. 'It's—Nash I wish to speak with. We're—er—friends. Close friends,' she added for good measure.

She knew her confident tone had fallen away as she brought out the last two words. The telephonist had noticed it too, she was sure. But before she could retrieve the situation, try to intimate to the girl that she would be in trouble if she didn't put her through, the way she thought any woman truly a close friend of the head of the Devereux Corporation might adopt, the girl was saying, almost purring as she said it, Perry thought:

'I'm sorry,' not sounding all that sorry, 'Mr Devereux must have forgotten to tell you—he flew to the States this morning.'

Feeling about as big as a ten-penny piece, Perry kept her composure only long enough to say, 'Oh dear, I've missed him. Never mind, I'll give him a tinkle when he gets back.'

She stumbled out of the telephone box, a tinge of red in her cheeks that the girl at the Devereux Corporation must have thought she was chasing Nash. Obviously if she was as close a friend as she's tried to make out, she would have known he had left the country.

She made her way back to work, her mind teeming with things she could have said. She hadn't even asked when he was coming back, though she realised she couldn't have very well, not after having pretended she had forgotten he was leaving for the States that day. A fine fool she'd already made of herself without adding to it by pretending she'd forgotten when he was coming home. The girl on the switchboard had rumbled her anyway, had known she wasn't really a friend of his, would more than likely have fobbed her off saying he didn't say when he would be returning.

Her problem loomed large in her mind throughout the rest of the day. She tried to hide that anything was worrying her, but when Madge looking up from her work suddenly said, 'Something still troubling you, Perry?' her voice for once serious, she realised her face must be very expressive.

'Nothing that can't be resolved,' she said after a moment's thought. If Madge could have helped, she might have told her, for often in the past they had exchanged confidences and she knew her to be the soul of discretion.

'Troubles shared . . .' Madge suggested, but Perry shook her head.

'Thanks anyway,' she smiled.

'I'll make you a cup of tea,' said Madge, and it sounded so comical the way she said it, just as though she thought that in the absence of a magic wand to dissolve Perry's troubles a cup of tea might do the trick, that they both laughed.

Madge left early, not without receiving a sly comment from Mr Ratcliffe about part-timers, but they both knew he didn't mean it. They had an admirable working arrangement. Mr Ratcliffe, thought of fondly by all his staff, was easy about time off, knowing that any one of them would drop everything and work until midnight if the occasion demanded it.

By the time Trevor's promised call came through, about ten minutes before she was due to go home, Perry had had time to reason, painful though it would be, that until she had this whole tangle sorted out, it might be better if she didn't see him so often.

'Sorry to be so late ringing,' he apologised. 'I've been out most of the day and only just got back.'

'That's all right.' There was nothing to forgive. Trevor worked as an insurance assessor and was often out of his office.

'I'd have rung you tonight before I went to see Mother,' he went on, and her heart warmed to him that not having a phone herself he would have put aside that he had no time for her landlady, would have rung asking to speak to her. Mrs Foster never minded calling her to the phone.

It was instinctive in Perry to be natural with Trevor, but as he chatted on, telling her about his day, his suspicions that the insured party he had seen was trying to lead him up the garden path, she was desperately trying to think up an excuse why she couldn't see him when he finally came round to that subject. At last he came to the end of how his claimant would have to get up early to fool him, and was asking the question she still hadn't got an answer to.

'We'll go to the cinema tomorrow night, shall we? I'll pick you up . . .'

'Er—actually,' she stalled him, 'we're rather busy at work at the moment.' Trust Mr Ratcliffe to walk by at precisely that second! He made a face that said, 'I'm the last to know?' and rudely Perry turned her back on him, part of her wanting to grin, for all the matter in hand was so very serious. 'Er—could we give tomorrow night a miss?' And weakening rapidly at the sulky silence the other end, 'We can go to the pictures another night.'

At home, she made herself a light meal, only picking at it before deciding she didn't want it. Never having time to read the morning edition, she couldn't settle either to read the paper she picked up every evening. Trevor had been huffy that she put her work before him and said if she couldn't see him tomorrow, he was tied up himself until Saturday.

Well, it was what she wanted, wasn't it? But it wasn't. Had he suggested seeing her on Thursday she knew she would have agreed. Now she was getting cold feet that he would ever propose at all. Oh, what a mess!

At seven she went downstairs to help Mrs Foster with the dress she was making. But at eight, having been invited to stay longer after Mrs Foster had declared she would learn more quickly if she did the next step herself when she had been put right on a facing she had cut incorrectly, Perry decided to go back to her flat. She didn't want Mrs Foster to see that same something in her that had prompted Madge to ask, 'Anything wrong?'

For a further hour she kicked against her ill luck that Nash Devereux was out of the country, knowing that she'd die before she would speak to that all-knowing voice on the Devereux Corporation switchboard again.

It was some time after nine when, fed up with her thoughts going the same round again and again, she decided action was the only answer. She couldn't verbally get in touch with Nash, just as she couldn't see a solicitor until that contact had been made with her paper marriage husband. What she could do, though, was write to him. If she wrote tonight, then whenever he got back, always hoping his visit to the States was for a few days only, and if she marked the envelope 'Strictly Private and Confidential', then he was bound to have it handed to him his first day back in business.

She got out her writing paper, musing that she didn't know where he lived. He no longer lived at the address shown on the marriage certificate, the house he had been born in. That house had been left to Lydia, his step-mother.

Perry headed the notepaper with her address, and just in case he wasn't a letter writer, knowing Mrs Foster wouldn't mind, put her phone number too. She didn't want him ringing her at work, everyone would know her secret within five minutes if he rang there.

'Dear——' she penned, and came to a full stop. A spark

of humour flickered briefly—and died. She didn't know him well enough to call him Nash, but it was too ridiculous to address the man she had married as 'Mr Devereux'. She added 'Nash' and came to another full stop as she tried to recall if apart from the ceremony when she'd said 'I, Perry, do take thee, Nash' she'd ever addressed him by any name at all.

The pen went slack in her hand and it was effortlessly, as though it was only yesterday, that she recalled that first meeting with Nash Devereux and all that had followed.

CHAPTER TWO

In her mind's eye Perry saw Nash Devereux the way he had been that first time she had clapped eyes on him—tall, immaculately suited, a cold, embittered look to him. A man she had thought then totally out of place on the small landing with its faded wallpaper outside her step-aunt's marriage bureau.

She had probably been looking a little grim herself, she thought, for she had been an exceedingly worried eighteen-year-old. She remembered how she had telephoned Sylvia that morning asking if she could come and see her in her lunch hour.

'What about?' Syvia had asked without too much enthusiasm.

'I can't really say over the phone,' she had answered, already aware that Sylvia wasn't in her most sympathetic frame of mind.

'Ralph, I suppose,' guessed Sylvia, bang on target. Perry had said nothing. 'I helped him out last time,' Ralph's sister had gone on. 'Don't expect . . .'

'If I could just come and see you,' Perry had said quickly, even then knowing it was hopeless. But who else was there to turn to? Everything that was of saleable value had been sold the last time, there wasn't an item of her mother's jewellery left. Nothing at all left that was likely to come anywhere near to realising the five thousand pounds that was the figure Ralph had last night confessed he owed to his bookmaker, his promise never to gamble again broken in the face of the compulsion that came over him.

'I'm busy right now,' Sylvia had said.

'Please!' she had heard herself pleading.

'Oh—come if you want to.' And with that ungracious invitation, Sylvia had put down the phone.

But there had still been hope in Perry's young heart when, counting every second until one o'clock, she had eventually left the place where she was employed as a trainee seamstress, and rushed round to the Perfect Partners Marriage Bureau Sylvia ran.

All hope in her had died when, rattling on Sylvia's office door on the first floor landing, she had found it locked. She had had to accept then that not only did Sylvia not want to see her, nor want to help Ralph, but she had deliberately, after agreeing to see her, gone out to avoid being drawn into what she must have guessed was some monetary crisis.

Not that she could blame her, Perry thought, turning disconsolately away from the door, barely aware of the tall figure of a man coming up the stairs. She had helped out the last time Ralph had got himself into trouble, though the amount then had been nowhere near the amount this time. Sylvia had sworn 'Never again' when she had handed over the money last time. That Ralph too had sworn 'Never again' when vowing he would never gamble again was without foundation, for within a very short space of time he had broken his vow. Why he consorted with the type of people who were threatening dire consequences if the five thousand he owed wasn't paid within two weeks, Perry didn't know—or perhaps she did. No bookmaking company of any repute would allow him so much credit.

She started down the stairs. Vaguely she heard the sound of the door she had tried being rattled, and turned three stairs down to offer, not very enthusiastically, she had to admit, 'Mrs Wainwright is at lunch.'

What kept her attention on the man she was afterwards never quite sure. Probably because he was the sort of man no one could overlook. Something in him had her still looking at him anyway when she meant to turn and go on her way.

It was then she noticed the cold, ruthless look of him, the look that said something had displeased him. It couldn't be just because he had been hoping to find the marriage bureau open and was put out because it wasn't, she found herself thinking—and then found she was wondering why he had called at a marriage bureau at all. Even with that sour expression on his face he had a certain something, she recognised that in him even if his air of there being little that surprised him made him a man she would have been terrified to date. As if she'd have the chance, she thought, and turned to carry on down the stairs.

His voice halted her, a pleasant voice she couldn't help thinking. It had a nice ring to it, for all there was a touch of grimness in it.

'It would appear we're both out of luck.'

She turned, about to put him right in the fewest of words that her visit to the marriage bureau was not for the business of finding herself a mate. But the sharp look that came to him suddenly took the words from her. She felt alarm at the way his stone-hard grey eyes flicked briefly over her before his look became calculating, a look that told her clearly he had thought of something, and that something had some connection with her.

'How old are you?'

The question was fired rapidly—so rapidly that she found herself answering, when all her instincts were telling her to run.

'Eighteen,' she said, and then began to obey her instincts. As she was about to turn away again that cool voice stopped her.

'You'll do,' he said, just as though, used as he was to making instant decisions, some problem had been solved, and that was an end to it.

'I'll do?' she queried, beginning to see why he needed her step-aunt's services. He must be some kind of a nut. No girl would willingly tie herself up to him, for all his certain something. 'Do for what?' she found herself asking, while her instinct to be away was becoming urgent.

He looked at her as though he thought she was being tiresome not to have kept up with him. 'I'll marry you,' he said distinctly.

'Marry me!' Her green eyes saucer-wide, she just stood and stared at him.

'Look, I haven't got time for pretence,' he snapped. 'You're here to find a partner, so am I.'

'I . . .' she began, then realised belatedly that she should never have turned back, and from somewhere found a coldness alien to her nature. 'No, thank you,' she said primly, and turned to do what she should have done earlier.

She had descended no more than two stairs when the voice above her, supremely confident, said, 'I'll make it worth your while.' Momentarily she halted, about to throw over her shoulder what he could do with his money. 'I'll give you five thousand pounds to go through a marriage ceremony with me,' he added, and as she heard the amount he was prepared to pay, the words she had been ready to fling at him promptly died in her throat.

Five thousand pounds! Ralph needed five thousand pounds if, to hear him talk, he wasn't to be dumped in the river in a cement overcoat. Her mouth slightly-open, Perry forced herself to turn and face the man who had just proposed that he be her husband, when what she wanted to do was take to her heels and run like fury.

'I thought that would get you,' the man said cynically.

'I . . .' she began, then as it came to her that she must be as mad as him to even think of doing what he was proposing, 'No,' she said firmly, and saw his lips twist in a disbelieving smile. Then he made another of those lightning decisions, making her wonder if he had even heard her refusal.

'We'll discuss the arrangements over lunch,' she was informed.

'But . . .' she began to protest, startled that he seemed to think the whole thing settled.

He moved, began to descend the stairs, and as he reached her she swallowed and moved too—and to her amazement found she was trotting along beside him on the pavement until they came to a restaurant that seemed to suit him.

Still feeling slightly stupefied that she didn't seem to be in charge of herself any more, she began to feel better on realising that not much harm could come to her with so many other people around. But her healthy appetite had long since disappeared, though rather than appear a ditherer she chose quickly from the menu, without thought to whether she was going to like what was placed before her.

Barely had the waiter gone than the man opposite her was introducing himself as Nash Devereux and enquiring her name. 'Perry Grainger,' she told him, her nerves settling down since for all there was an aggressive look to him, he no longer appeared to be the crazy individual she had first thought him.

'Right,' he said, 'I need to have paper proof that I have a wife—and though it's obvious since you're only eighteen that you feel—security—is more important than that cosy little word called love,' dear heaven, he was sounding cynical, she couldn't help thinking, 'your reasons for wanting a husband are of no concern to me.'

She bit down the urge to tell him she didn't want a husband at all—well, not until she fell in love anyway. But she could see he would scoff at her if she made any such remark, and could well come back with: what was she doing having lunch with him in that case? And then she recalled he had said he needed to have *paper* proof that he had a wife, and was glad her wits hadn't completely deserted her.

Hope sprang within her and with it sudden daring. Dared she, if it was to be one of those name only things, dared she commit herself to marrying him, to taking the five thousand pounds that was so vitally important to Ralph? Not giving herself time to think further, she was blurting out:

'You said you needed paper proof,' and jumping in before her courage failed, 'Does that mean you don't want to be married in the—er—real sense of the word?'

Her pale cheeks were crimson as she forced the last words through her lips. But Nash Devereux gave her very little time to feel embarrassed.

'God forbid!' shot from him, the violence of his words underlining their sincerity. 'It's a necessary evil, no more.' Then, his look sharp, 'If you have any idea in your head of making more out of this than five thousand, forget it. I shan't want you round my neck after the ceremony.'

Her sensitivities wounded that any man could speak to her so, be so aggressive to the point of rudeness, Perry wanted to tell him what he could do with his five thousand, tell him she didn't want it. She checked. But she did want it, and if all she had to do to get it was to put up with a few of his insulting remarks until the ceremony was performed and they went their separate ways, then since clearly no help would be forthcoming from Sylvia and there being no one else to turn to, she would have to swallow her pride and take it. But scarey as she found him she couldn't resist a pride-wounded retort of:

'That goes for me too, only double!'

'Good,' he said briefly, and would have gone straight away into giving her information needed for the marriage. But though only eighteen she might be, and desperate to have the money for Ralph as she was, there was a streak of caution in her that had her questioning before he could continue:

'Why is it so important that you can produce a certificate to say you're married?'

His expression was hard as he looked away. Then quickly his laser-beamed look was back on her, piercing through her, everything about him telling her she could mind her own damn business. And while she looked back at him, her eyes wide and apprehensive at the no-bones words she had been expecting, the rough words didn't come.

'Are you alone in the world?' he enquired, his face stern.

There was Ralph. But loving Ralph as if he was the father who had died when she was a baby, she couldn't tell this hard-eyed stranger anything about him. Some fear gnawed at her that he might change his mind about the money if he knew it was to be spent on settling Ralph's gambling debts.

'My parents are dead,' she told him, her voice low.

'So you have no one to look out for you,' he stated consideringly. 'Though you must have your head screwed on the right way to be sitting here with me now, for all you're young enough to still bear cradle marks.'

And when she had thought he had decided she could run for her explanation of why he needed that marriage certificate, he unbent sufficiently to tell her:

'My father died two months ago,' and at her look of instant sympathy, 'It was expected.' His jaw firmed, and she saw then that expected or not it had hit him hard. 'What wasn't expected, not by me at any rate,' he went on, 'was that my father would disinherit me if I wasn't married within three months after his death.'

Perry gasped. So that was the reason! He had another month in which to fulfil the terms of his father's will, or lose his inheritance. She had not idea how much money was involved. But if he was the only son he had every right to expect his father to leave him everything. Unless there was some good reason why he shouldn't.

'Why would he want to do that?' she couldn't keep from asking—and received another look that told her he thought it none of her business. 'I'm sorry,' she apologised at once, having seen from his look that he thought he had given her sufficient reason for him needing to be married.

But again he surprised her. Though afterwards she was able to realise that his only motive in telling her anything else was in order that she should see that when he had said marriage was a necessary evil and that he didn't want her round his neck afterwards, he had meant exactly that.

'Enter the wicked stepmother,' he said humourlessly, and as Perry ploughed her way through her meal, she learned, from what he said and what he didn't say—his cold cynicism filling in any gaps—that Nash Devereux knew all about women and then some, and the women he had met, gone around with, had left him with no rosy view of her sex.

Lydia, his stepmother, had been his girl-friend before she had married his father, Joel Devereux. Nash, she gathered from the way he spoke, had no illusions about women, having seen from an early age the succession of prize-hunters his father had entertained since his divorce from his mother. Lydia, thinking Nash more enamoured of her than he was, had lost complete control of her temper one night when no marriage proposal was forthcoming, and had furiously told him if he wouldn't marry her, then she intended to marry his father. Perry could only gather what Nash had told her in answer to that—nothing very pleasant, she thought, imagining that he would be terrifying if he too had lost his temper. He had then had to watch while Lydia made a play for Joel, had tried to tell his father that Lydia was only after his money. But Joel wouldn't hear a word against her, and anything Nash said was taken to be sour grapes because Lydia preferred the much older man.

'So she married him,' Nash said, not a flicker of emotion in his face as he went on to tell her how his father's good living prior to and after his marriage had resulted in his first heart attack. 'He should have let up then, but he wouldn't. He was too anxious to show that bitch he could keep pace with any man half his age.'

He broke off when the waiter came to serve the last course, and Perry knew, for all he wasn't showing it, that there was pain in Nash that any attempt he made to get his father to change his pace of life had been seen as him hankering for Lydia and not wanting her to be happy in her life with her husband.

'I couldn't bear to watch what she was doing to him,' Nash continued when the waiter had gone. 'I spent more and more time at the Works,' his expression became granite as he said, 'and that played nicely into Lydia's hands. On the day Joel was buried, purring with the pleasure of being able to tell me so, she told me she had suggested to him that I worked far too hard. That what I needed was a wife so I could enjoy life as they did, play and be happy as they were, otherwise she was dreadfully afraid I would drive myself into an early grave.'

'So your father, believing her, changed his will?' It sounded incredible, but then, thank goodness, she hadn't ever met anyone like the woman Nash was describing.

'I knew he intended to so Lydia should inherit the house. He altered it—and how!—a few weeks before he died,' Nash said, his eyes flint-hard. 'He couldn't know I'd told his dear wife the night she'd been angling for me to propose, that not only did I not want to marry her, but that there wasn't a woman breathing I'd sacrifice my freedom for—I left her in no doubt that I meant it.'

'Oh!' The exclamation left Perry at the bitterness in him. 'But—but that's what you'll have to do if you want to claim your inheritance, isn't it? Within the next month too.'

She wished he would smile, just once. She thought he might look rather pleasant if he allowed those wonderful teeth she had glimpsed when he spoke to have an airing. But no, his face was a cold mask as he answered:

'It's what I intend to do. I left my lawyers only a short while ago—the will is watertight. You and I will marry on Friday.'

Perry had been late getting back to work, but for once that hardly bothered her. Her head was teeming with everything that had happened, been said, her impressions many and varied, but only one clear fact loomed large. On Friday, three days from now, she was to present herself at the register office where once Nash had the means to prove he was married he would hand over the five thousand pounds.

It hadn't taken long for him to jot down her full name and all the details he thought he would need. He had asked for her phone number too just in case a need arose for him to contact her before Friday. It was then she had to confess she had a stepfather, having to ask him not to let slip any of what she was doing should Ralph answer the phone.

'Don't you get on with your step-relative either?' Nash had asked. But she had kept quiet. To say Ralph was a love—when he wasn't gambling—might have Nash wondering why she had been looking for a marriage partner at all if her home life was so happy.

Many times before Friday came Perry was to wonder if she was as crazy as she had at first thought him to be. But as she looked at Ralph as he sat slumped over the fire on Thursday evening, misery, dejection personified, her heart went out to the man who had so loved her mother he had gone utterly to pieces when she had died twelve months ago. She knew then that if Nash *had* been serious, and only now was she beginning to doubt it, then if that was the only way to get the five thousand she was going to go through with it.

Though longing as she was to see a return of the laughing, leg pulling Ralph, that small percentage of doubt that Nash might not be at the register office tomorrow, no five thousand pounds forthcoming, kept her from telling Ralph that soon his worries would be over. As it was she was racking her brains to think up some good explanation of where she had got the money from. As unhappy as Ralph undoubtedly was, worried out of his mind, he would have a fit for certain if he had the smallest inclination of what she was contemplating on his behalf.

On Friday, solely to keep Ralph from suspecting that this Friday was different from any other Friday, she dressed exactly as she would if she intended going to work. Since she was still a junior in her job, seeming to spend half her time on the floor picking up pins, trousers were the most practical apparel.

'I'll try and get home early tonight,' she promised when Ralph glanced up as she went into the kitchen, the deeply etched grooves under his eyes telling her he had slept not a wink. Impulsively she went and put her arms around his bent shoulders, giving him a tight squeeze and having to hold hard on the urge to tell him everything would be all right. 'Try not to worry, love,' she said instead, which was no comfort at all, she knew, as he lifted his hand absently to pat her.

'Drink your tea,' he instructed automatically. 'If you don't hurry you're going to be late.'

Unable to tell him she was having a day off from her holiday quota, Perry swallowed a hasty cup of tea and left the house at her normal time, knowing she had a couple of hours to kill before going to see if Nash Devereux had been as sincere as he had seemed to be.

She was on her fourth cup of coffee in her third café when, glancing once more at her watch, she saw it showed the same time as it had ten minutes ago. In a flash she was on her feet. Not having wanted to look like a bride who had been left stranded if Nash didn't turn up, though anyone less bridelike in her old baggy jacket and trousers she couldn't imagine, she had calculated on finishing her coffee and leaving a sedate two-minute stroll to the register office. As it was, having run all the way she was red-faced, breathless and three minutes late when she got there, relief mixing with apprehensive butterflies that Nash Devereux had turned up. And from the way he was angrily pacing up and down, a none too sweet Nash Devereux.

'I'm sorry I'm late,' she apologised quickly, seeing he looked ready to blast her, and all too well aware of how shabbily turned out she must appear dressed as she was when he was in a faultlessly tailored suit. 'I'm sorry I couldn't dress up—I didn't want Ralph to know.'

At her reminder that she too, or so he thought, had a step-relative she didn't get on with, some of the impatience left him.

'You're here,' he said tautly, 'that's all that matters.' And without waiting another moment he was hurrying her to where the registrar, his assistant and a couple of roped-in witnesses were standing.

Perry supposed the registrar must be used to nervous, stammering brides, as her responses were uttered with none of the firm, confident tone she heard coming from the man beside her, for the registrar smiled encouragingly at her from time to time. And then it was all over. She had a wedding ring on one hand, while her other hand was being shaken, and, confused, she heard the registrar refer to her as Mrs Devereux. Nash then led her out into an ante-room, and they were alone.

She thought she ought to say something, but she hadn't a clue what one was supposed to say in the circumstances. He didn't appear to have anything to say either. But when she would have gone through the door that led to the street, his hand on her arm stayed her.

'We'll keep this matter private, I think,' he said coolly, and dipped his hand into his jacket pocket and pulled out a bulky envelope. 'You've kept your part of the bargain—here's mine,' he said. And so there would be no argument, he opened the envelope, showed her the contents, new crisp notes, and handed it to her.

Still speechless, her insides not a scrap settled, Perry took the envelope from him, embarrassment threatening to swamp her as she hastily pushed the envelope and its contents in her bag out of sight. Then just as though he had satisfactorily completed a business deal, which afterwards she began to realise was all it was to him, Nash extended his hand.

'I'll escort you to the pavement, but we'll say goodbye here.'

Perry found her hand in his firm, cool clasp. 'Er—thank you,' she said, feeling idiotic as she said it.

'Goodbye,' he answered, and it was final.

Afterwards, another unwanted coffee in front of her, but a much-needed chair beneath her, she could hardly credit that she had actually married him. She took a surreptitious look in her bag, half expecting the envelope Nash had given her to be a figment of her imagination. But no, there it was. Hastily she closed her bag.

For a further half hour she sat there. And gradually, as thoughts of Ralph began to filter through, she started to feel better, even a little pleased with herself.

Leaving the café, unable to go home yet, she walked and walked, the feel of the ring new on her finger reminding her that she had better get rid of it before she got home. All saleable jewellery in the house had gone; she didn't want Ralph asking questions about this expensive piece of platinum. As she neared the river, without a second thought, though giving a careful look round to see if she was being observed, the ring was off her finger, meeting its watery end with barely a plop.

Only then, her small confidence back with her, did it dawn on her that with so much else on her mind, she hadn't given thought to question Nash as to what they should do about a divorce. It came to her then for the first

time that with the way he felt about women, the question
of divorce obviously hadn't bothered him. The Equator
would freeze over before he would want to remarry.

By the time she arrived home, to find Ralph still
slumped on a kitchen chair just as though he hadn't moved
all day, Perry had her story ready to tell him.

'I told you not to worry,' she said gaily, and while
Ralph tried to dredge up a smile that something good
must have happened for her that she would look so pleased,
Perry rushed on, 'I've got the five thousand for you.'

Maybe because he wanted to believe it, Ralph had
taken without question that she had gone to see his sister
Sylvia earlier in the week and today Sylvia had rung
through to say she had sold some shares and could let her
have the money.

That Ralph was overjoyed and immediately dropped
ten years was an understatement. 'I never for a moment
thought she'd help. She swore she wouldn't after the last
time,' he said, having danced Perry round the kitchen. 'I
must ring and thank her straight away.'

'No!' The word left her sharply. Fear was uppermost
she would have to tell him what she'd done, the burden of
guilt he would carry to know she had done it for him. 'I—
well—well, to tell you the truth,' she said, seeing at once
that some explanation had to be made, 'Sylvia was—
er—a little cross about it.'

Ralph knew his sister very well, it seemed, for all they
had never been all that close. 'She neither wants to see or
hear from me ever again, is that it?'

She hated having to lie to him, but knowing Ralph
couldn't have loved her more if she had been his own
daughter, she thought she knew best what he could live
with better—that his sister didn't want to know him or
that his stepdaughter had married a stranger to settle his
gambling debt.

'Well, not until some of the money has been paid back,'

she invented on the spur of the moment, not wanting to be the cause of a permanent rift between the blood relatives, for all they rarely met. 'I've arranged for us to pay the money back by monthly instalments.' Perhaps she and Ralph could use it to have that holiday abroad he was hankering after, her mind went on.

But the holiday abroad never came to fruition, she thought sadly. Nor had there been time for Ralph to make even the first payment. For before she had been married to Nash for a month, Ralph had died as a result of being injured when the driver of the bus he had been on had suffered heart failure, and the bus went out of control and crashed into a brick wall.

The sound of Mrs Foster below riddling her fire, something she did every night last thing, had Perry coming back to the present with a start. Her eyes fell to her writing paper, nothing else written after her 'Dear Nash'.

She gripped her pen once more, realising that if she didn't keep her concentration on the job in hand she would never get to bed. That letter had to be written tonight ready to post in the morning.

Several direct and to the point phrases presented themselves in her head, but she hesitated. The trouble was, for all she was married to him, she barely knew Nash Devereux. It would look well if her direct approach made his hackles rise and he dug his heels in. Though why he should, she couldn't think, and anyway, he was pretty direct himself, wasn't he? Or had been in all his dealing with her.

Yet still she hesitated. If Nash *wanted* to be free he would somehow have found where she had moved to after Ralph's death. Fear gripped her that he could well refuse to arrange for them to be quietly divorced somewhere. And another half an hour went by and many ripped up sheets of paper before she finally settled for, 'Dear Nash, If it's all right with you I should like to be free. Would you let me know as soon as possible if you are agreeable to a divorce. Yours sincerely, Perry Grainger. P.S. I've put my landlady's phone number and am known as Miss Grainger.'

Quickly she folded the single sheet of paper and slipped it into its 'Strictly Private and Confidential' envelope, knowing if she stopped to re-read what she had written that too would be torn up, another attempt to be made.

She went to bed, aware that she would know little rest until her letter had been posted.

CHAPTER THREE

PERRY overslept the next morning, which was just as well, she thought, as hurrying to work she slipped her letter to Nash in the post box. Had there been time she knew very well she would have been tempted to scrap what she had written and start again. She continued on her way musing, well, at least now she had actually done something in an attempt to get the ball rolling. All she had to do now was to wait for Nash to come back from the States. He would contact her then, she felt sure. And then she and Trevor . . .

A week later she was still waiting. Anxious, racing home each night hoping for a letter, afraid to go out in case Nash rang and she missed him, when no word came she fell back on the thought that he must still be abroad.

She had gone out on Saturday. Not only did she not want to put Trevor off in case Nash did ring, but since her last conversation with Trevor, over the telephone, had not been all that satisfactory, she was eager to see him to make up. Trevor had been equally eager to see her, and she felt a glow inside that he wasn't holding a grudge because she had put him off last Wednesday. So happy had she been, in fact, that any thought of cooling the situation between them until her annulment came through went right out of her head, and she dated him on Sunday and Monday as well.

But by the time Wednesday came around and still no word from Nash Devereux, her anxieties were beginning to show through.

'Something worrying you?' Trevor enquired. They were sitting outside her flat in his car after an evening spent at the cinema.

'No, nothing, nothing at all,' she denied, half of her ready to panic that after several hours spent in her company he must have realised she wasn't her usual self, while the other half of her was wondering if this wasn't just the opportunity to tell him everything.

'Is it something I've said?' he insisted, plainly not believing her when she said nothing was wrong.

She looked at him, the light from a street lamp making his fair hair seem darker, softening the sharp lines of his features. 'I . . .' she began, and didn't get any further.

'Perhaps it's something I've not said,' he interrupted.

She heard the smile in his voice and the moment was lost when she might have gathered all her courage and told him. She knew then that he was referring to the fact that he hadn't followed up from his intimation over a week ago that he was considering asking her to marry him.

'Bear with me, darling,' he said, his voice still smiling, confident he knew her answer once he had everything sorted out in his mind. 'Only last night Mother was saying exactly what I've already told you, that I need to be very sure before I commit myself.'

A mixture of emotions beset Perry. She wasn't sure she liked the way Trevor was taking a long detached looked at the prospect of them being married. The way he was not allowing anything of impetuous love to rule his head. Any more than she liked the fact that he had obviously been discussing her—and discussing marrying her—with his mother.

Then all the guilt of her secret flooded in and she felt further guilt heaped on her head that she should for a moment take exception to anything he did. With his parents' marriage as an example, the constant record Mrs Coleman played on divorce, no wonder he was taking his time in making up his mind. And anyway, hadn't she already decided she didn't want him to ask her to marry him until she was free?

But ready as she was to forgive him any slight, real or imaginary, she found there was something in her, some sore pride, which had her sharper with him when he pulled her into his arms and showed every sign that if mentally he wasn't yet ready to commit himself to marriage, then his physical being had no objection to trying to anticipate that state of affairs.

'No!' she said, more sharply than she would otherwise have done had not her pride been ruffled.

'Oh, come on, Perry,' he tried to coax, 'we know each other well enough by now—we love each other, don't we?'

Perry was firm then as she had been on other occasions, though she hardly knew why. True, she owned, Trevor had succeeded in niggling her, but she had enjoyed his kisses before.

'I think I'll go in,' she said, struggling out of his arms, amazed at the thought that had just popped into her head; the thought that maybe she couldn't let herself go with Trevor, or any of the boy-friends she had had before him, because for all her paper marriage was just that and no more, deep, deep down her subconscious recognised she was still married!

Reluctantly, with bad grace, he let her go. 'I'll ring you,' he said, and didn't wait until she was in the house before he had driven away.

She sighed, her thoughts a jumble as she went upstairs to her flat. She wanted peace of mind, but what chance of that was there with on one hand Trevor on the brink of proposing, her wanting to say yes with her dreadful secret yet to be revealed, and Nash Devereux taking his time in contacting her?

A kind of desperation gripped her, and she knew if she didn't hear from him soon she would, regardless of that all-knowing voice on the Devereux Corporation switchboard, be ringing them and demanding to know his telephone number in the States. She couldn't go on like this much longer.

The next morning found her feeling a little brighter, and with Madge's unfailing good humour she was a good deal lifted by the time it came to go home. Trevor hadn't rung, but then he didn't every day. Hope was with her as her feet sped homewards, only one thought in her mind—to hurry indoors and see if a letter had come for her from Nash.

'No paper tonight?'

Joe, the newsvendor with whom she always stopped to have a word every night, had her realising her mind had been so taken up with the thought of the letter that could be waiting for her, she had for the first time ever passed his stand without picking up her paper.

'Sorry, Joe,' she said, quickly retracing her steps, 'miles away.'

'Hope he's worth it,' Joe winked, as his grubby gnarled hands exchanged newsprint for change.

'He is,' she said, because it was expected of her. ' 'Night, Joe,' she offered, her urgent need to get home too much for her to stand chatting.

But disappointment awaited her. Mrs Foster always put her mail on the hall table, but there was nothing there. Even so, as Mrs Foster came limping out on her way with something she was taking to the dustbins at the rear, Perry couldn't hold back her enquiry of:

'No post for me, Mrs Foster?'

'No, love,' said Mrs Foster, her motherly eyes fond on the lovely girl who had rented the upstairs rooms for six years now. 'Were you expecting something, Perry?'

'It'll probably come tomorrow,' she answered, trying to look unconcerned. 'It isn't anything important.'

Not much it isn't, she thought, in her flat, her meal eaten more from habit than because she felt hungry. She'd be a nervous wreck if she didn't hear from Nash Devereux soon.

She took the used crockery into her kitchen, and since

she had nothing planned that night dumped everything in the sink to be washed up later, feeling the need to relieve some of her tension with a read of the paper. Going back into her sitting room she picked up the paper and sank down into her one easy chair, musing on the possibility of writing to Nash again, only this time marking the envelope 'Urgent, Please Forward'. That wouldn't do, she thought, opening the paper. She didn't want him to get the idea that her wish to be free was so terribly urgent. She . . .

Her thoughts stopped dead, her mind going temporarily blank. For there, bang on the front page, was a picture of Nash Devereux arriving at London Airport, a gorgeous-looking female hanging on to him as if her life depended on it. But it wasn't so much the picture that had her eyes going wide, the knowledge that he was back penetrating, but what was threatening to have her eyes popping out of her head was the newspaper headline!

She had written asking how he felt about a divorce. He had neither written nor telephoned. But here, here in black and white, she had her answer. For the caption in large print read, 'SORRY ELVIRA', that must be the girl in the picture, 'NASH DEVEREUX WANTS RECONCILIATION WITH HIS WIFE'.

Panicking madly, terrified of seeing her own name in print, since there were not too many Perry Bethia Graingers around for Trevor not to read her secret in the paper before she could get to tell him personally, she hastily read on.

Shaken rigid, she read that Nash had gone to the States endeavouring to tie up a big deal. News that his visit had been successful had broken after his plane back to England had taken off. At the airport he had been met by not only Elvira Newman, his latest girl-friend, but had also been besieged by a whole host of pressmen. He had refused to give any interviews at the airport saying he would see the journalists at his office later.

Perry saw then that back at his office he must have

flipped through any of his mail that looked important, her own 'Strictly Private and Confidential' missive among them.

Still terrified of seeing her name, she scanned quickly through the report of the high-powered meetings he had had in America, his success in reaching a satisfactory outcome, of contracts being signed, until she came to the last few paragraphs.

All questions on the business deal out of the way one reporter had thought to ask if there was any significance in Elvira Newman meeting him at the airport. To which Nash had countered:

'Significance?'

'Are things serious between the two of you?' the reporter had pressed, knowing full well that Nash was aware of what he was asking, but nowhere near to guessing the bombshell just about to be dropped.

According to the reporter Nash had taken his time in answering, as though savouring every moment, until he at last announced, 'How could they be—when I'm hoping for a reconciliation with my wife?'

Perry wasn't breathing at all as she read the questions thrown at him in the uproar that had followed, expecting every moment to see her name. The 'We didn't even know you were married much less estranged.' The who, when, where, questions that were fired in rapid succession.

Panic departed and relief gushed as she saw, for all the badgering he received, that Nash wasn't prepared to add anything to what he had already said.

She read the report through again, but couldn't understand it. And gradually anger began to take the place of fear as she asked the question, why? Why—why had he done this?

More and more convinced he had received her letter, she began to hate him that when he could so easily have lifted a telephone to acquaint her with his answer, he had chosen this way to let her know the arrangement suited him very well as it stood, thank you.

That he spoke of wanting a reconciliation was just so much hogwash, she thought furiously. They had never been conciled in the first place! No, tired from his negotiations, jet-lagged probably, he had been caught on the raw that she was the one to want to be free, when it had always been Casanova Nash Devereux's right to tell his females bye-bye.

Trevor Coleman hardly entered Perry's thoughts as over and over she railed against Nash Devereux and the dreadful thing he had done. Did the fact that he had refused to give her name mean he had rumbled that she didn't want any publicity? He was sharp enough to find ten different reasons for her writing to him rather than going off on her own bat and filing for divorce, she realised too late. Though she didn't find anything to thank him for that he had kept her name to himself; she felt too angry to thank him for anything.

On impulsive temper she slipped on her jacket and left the house to find the nearest telephone box. Mrs Foster would have been pleased to let her use her telephone, she knew, but what she had to say to Nash Devereux would be for no one's ears other than his.

Ten minutes later, angry, frustrated and hardly able to wait for tomorrow when she would ring the Devereux Corporation—and to hell with his shrewd telephonist— Perry let herself into her flat cursing the day the Post Office ever instigated ex-directory numbers. She had felt just in the mood to blast his eardrums, nothing of the eighteen-year-old scaredy-cat she had been the last time she had seen him about her. But even telling Directory Enquiries she had urgent need of his number hadn't relaxed the rule that ensured he didn't have any Tom, Dick or Harry calling him.

By the time morning came, she was beginning to think

perhaps it was just as well she hadn't been able to get through to last night. She would have gone for him hammer and tongs, that was for sure. But in the light of day, for all there was anger inside at what he had done, she was able to reason more calmly that she might fare better in getting Nash to agree to a quiet divorce if she stayed controlled rather than go for him spitting fire.

At half past ten, Perry put down the garment she was putting the finishing touches to and told Madge she was nipping out for a few minutes.

'Get me a packet of biscuits while you're out,' was Madge's unwanted request. 'I don't think I'm going to last until lunchtime.'

Not sure how she was going to feel after her phone call, and more than a little apprehensive before she started, Perry purchased Madge's biscuits before she went to the phone box, slipping them into her portmanteau-size handbag that weighed a ton, but which she found essential.

'Devereux Corporation,' said that well remembered voice.

'Mr Devereux, please,' said Perry smartly.

'I'll put you through to his secretary. Who's calling, please?'

Wanting to protest that she didn't want to speak to his secretary, she was suddenly disquieted by the thought that she didn't want any one to know her name either. 'Er— Miss Smith,' she said, and could have groaned out loud that that was the best she could come up with.

'Just one moment, Miss Smith,' said the voice she was sure had recognised her from the time before. And then a different female voice was saying she was Mr Devereux's secretary, and could she help her.

'I'm sure you can.' Perry put a smile into her voice, ready to try charming her way to get to speak to Nash Devereux if that was the only way it could be achieved, and really pushing it. 'I'd like to speak to Nash, please.'

'I'm sorry, Miss Smith,' her own charm was bounced back as she was politely headed off. 'Mr Devereux isn't taking calls or seeing anyone today. If you would like to leave a message I'll see he gets it straight away.'

About to insist on speaking to him, she recognised the hint that said it was more than the secretary dared do to put her through against her employer's instructions.

'It's not important,' she said, and put down the phone.

I won't be beaten, I won't! she fumed as she paced angrily away from the phone box. She could go on like this *ad infinitum*, trying to speak to Nash and getting fobbed off every time. Besides which, she wanted this whole thing sorted out today. Trevor was sure to ring today as he hadn't rung yesterday. She owed it to him to get it all settled.

It was as she went back to her seat after handing Madge her biscuits that the idea came of going along to the Devereux Corporation and waiting there until he came out. He was in the building, his secretary had as good as said so. All she had to do was to watch and wait for him to appear and then go up to him. He didn't want to be reconciled, she was sure of that, so he would have to stop and speak to her, wouldn't he? He wouldn't want to risk her taking him up on what he had told the press; she was on a winner there and no mistake.

She became briefly sidetracked as she visualised life with that hard, cold individual she had married and shuddered at the thought. She would go into a convent sooner! One thing was certain, though, she wasn't going to write to him again only to have to wait and read her reply in the evening paper. Abruptly she stood up—so abruptly, Madge left her absorption with her digestive biscuit and looked at her questioningly.

'Do you know where Mr Ratcliffe is?' Perry asked, her mind made up.

'Try the counting house,' Madge joked, then seeing the determined look on her face, 'It looks as though the problem you've been nursing quietly for the past week has just come to crisis point. Count me as one of your friends if you're having trouble with Trevor.'

Madge didn't like Trevor, Perry knew, but she also knew what Madge was really saying without wishing to pry was that in any sort of trouble she could count on her support.

'Thanks, Madge,' she said gratefully, 'I can handle it myself, but I need the rest of the day off.'

Her affection for Mr Ratcliffe grew that after one look at her serious face; perhaps because he could see it wasn't for any trivial matter she wanted so many hours off, he agreed without question.

Walking away from him, she caught sight of herself in a mirror near the door, and it was then she paused, her urgent need to get along to the Devereux Corporation temporarily suspended. She recalled without effort the elegantly turned out women seen photographed with her husband, and while her fine checked trouser suit she had made over twelve months ago was still smart, she knew suddenly that when the confrontation with Nash came she would feel far more able to keep her end up in his sophisticated company if she was dressed as elegantly as some of the females he squired around.

A few more minutes' delay wouldn't matter, she was thinking as her feet headed homewards. After all, she might have hours to wait as it was.

Her confidence took an upswing as she checked her appearance before leaving her flat for the second time that morning. Gone was the casually attired girl with honey-gold hair left free. In her place was an elegant young woman dressed in a fine wool dress of burnt orange with matching coat, her hair dressed in a classic knot and topped by the smartest rounded-domed hat in an autumn bronze that complimented her hair to perfection. Her portmanteau of a handbag just didn't go with the outfit, so she took a few more moments transferring a few essentials into a more fitting brown leather handbag.

She couldn'd help the smile that curved her lightly made up mouth, as without vanity she decided she might well be worth a second look, and for all Nash Devereux had no time for a wife, if the press reports were to be believed he was not averse to viewing the opposite sex.

Her confidence marginally dimmed as she reached the Devereux Corporation building, and butterflies began inside her giving the lie to the outwardly supremely confident being she wanted to appear. She halted, realising that dressed as she was she was going to attract too much attention if she stood outside for hour after hour.

The decision made for her, there being not even a café opposite the building she could sit in and use for a vantage point, she pushed open the plate glass doors, her eyes seeking and finding several comfortable-looking chairs, an admirable place to wait, she thought.

But she had delayed too long in moving over to one of them. 'Can I help you, madam?' The smart receptionist's enquiry was something totally unprepared for.

'Er—' Perry managed, approaching the desk automatically since it had never been her way to raise her voice unduly. 'Er—' she said, and before her thoughts were in any sort of order found she was saying, 'I'd like to see Mr Devereux.'

'I'm afraid Mr Devereux is tied up for the rest of the day,' the receptionist was answering while Perry's brain was waking up to the fact that, idiot that she was, having now stated who it was she wanted to see she couldn't very well now take a seat and wait for him to appear. 'If you would like to leave a message?' the girl was continuing.

'I think he'll see me.' Perry smiled one of her best smiles, then as casually as she could glanced around to see if

anyone was in earshot. Then lowering her voice and
hoping the girl would think she was confiding rather than
realise she wanted as few people as possible to overhear,
'Would you tell him his wife is here?'

The effect on the girl was dramatic. Shock instantly
ousted the look that said nobody got past her without her
say-so. 'I . . .' she began, before quickly gathering her wits
about her, her come-to-office smile struggling to get
through. 'If you wouldn't mind waiting a moment, Miss—
Mrs Devereux,' she said, obviously having read the evening paper just as Perry had, and trying fast to overcome
this latest development.

Perry thought she was half way to believing she was
who she said she was, though she was grateful that the girl
must still be nursing some doubt that she kept her voice
down when she picked up the phone and relayed the message to someone that Mr Devereux's wife was here to see
him.

She gathered the receptionist must first have spoken to
Nash's secretary, and felt her heart thumping when she
repeated her message, and realised that the girl was in all
probability now speaking with Nash.

She could have no idea what he was saying, but knew
that, though stubborn in her need to see him, her pride
would take a terrible blow if he was advising the girl to
tell her to get lost.

'Yes,' the girl answered. 'Yes, I'll do that, Mr Devereux.
Would you excuse me a moment, please?'

Perry tried to keep her face, looking unconcerned when
placing her hand over the mouthpiece the girl pulled the
phone away from her ear. She looked flushed, she thought,
and since Nash was obviously still holding on, she hoped
the receptionist's heightened colour was caused by the fact
that she had been speaking to the mighty chief himself,
rather than from any rude question he was waiting for the
answer from.

'I'm sorry, Mrs Devereux,' she said, her smile nowhere near as bright as it had been, 'but may I have your first name?'

This time there was no time for Perry to look round to see if anyone else was in earshot. But, terrified there might be some pressman lurking near, that her name could be splashed all over the front page of tonight's paper, she rapidly decided that having got this far to take the coward's way out and take to her heels, as every instinct urged, was not on. Striving manfully for a slightly humorous tone, just as though she thought it mildly amusing that her husband should take such precautions not to have his day interrupted by any bogus Mrs Devereux, she said quietly:

'Would you ask my—husband—if the initials P.B.G. mean anything to him?' and waited while the message was relayed.

She saw relief on the girl's face, a more natural smile showing itself as she replaced the phone. 'Mr Devereux said you wouldn't know where his office is. If you'd like to come with me I'll take you up.'

On the way in the lift Perry tried to get her thoughts into order. She wanted to see Nash. It was important she should see him; they had a vital matter to discuss. But she was feeling so shaky inside that all she was capable of thinking was that soon, after not so much as catching a glimpse of Nash Devereux in six whole years, she would soon be face to face with the man who had handed over five thousand pounds and looked as though to say if he never saw her again it would be too soon. All she could hope was that the six years in between had made him more approachable than he had been then.

She stepped out of the lift, turning with the receptionist, and went with her down a long hall. They stopped at one of the doors, the girl tapped lightly, then turned, evidently expecting Perry to precede her into the room.

Telling herself her feet didn't want to go the other way, trying to remember how angry she had been last night, reminding herself strongly that she was no longer afraid of Nash Devereux, that her happiness and Trevor's depended on the outcome of this meeting, Perry was suddenly filled with the light of battle. She went in.

CHAPTER FOUR

But it was not into Nash's office she entered. Nor did the receptionist stay longer than to introduce his busy-looking secretary, Karen Taylor, who rose from her chair. She was through the door almost before she had finished shaking hands with the blonde-haired Karen.

'Mr Devereux will be . . .' Karen began.

But what Mr Devereux would be was never heard. For the sound of the other door in the room opening had her breaking off, and two pairs of eyes went to see the tall, dark-haired man who stood there.

And it was at that moment, her eyes meeting grey eyes full on, eyes that showed an infinitesimal astonishment, quickly cancelled, that Perry's insides started to feel as though they belonged to anyone but her. Straight away she recognised him, a few strands of silver at his temples that hadn't been there before. A smile started to break as he left his position by the door and strode over to her, the only other unrecognised thing about him, for never had she seen him smile.

His smile she found weakening, but it did her tummy no good whatsoever to have her heart join in the free-for-all when he put an arm about her and she felt his lips cool on her cheek.

'My darling,' he said, warmth for her in his voice she had never heard before either, 'this is an unexpected pleasure.'

And before she could twist out of his hold, the arm about her shoulders was forcing her across the thick carpeting towards the door that must lead to his office. That arm still firm about her as he threw at Karen:

'Hold all my calls. I don't want to be disturbed. As you

know, it isn't every day my lovely wife comes to see me.'

In the few seconds it had taken for Nash to guide her across the carpet, the moments it took for him to have her safely closeted in his inner sanctum, Perry's emotions had undergone a dramatic change. No longer afraid of him, her uppermost feeling was anger at the charade he had played out there.

'How dare you?' she blazed, struggling out of his arm, for he had made no move to let her go. And it did nothing for her anger that his grey eyes suddenly lit with interest as they flicked over her. That interest added to as his gaze returned to her eyes and he saw the fury sparking there.

'Who would have thought,' he drawled laconically, if he recognised she was angry paying no heed to it, 'that you would turn out to be such a swan?'

For a moment Perry was floored that he was ignoring her fury, what he said sufficiently sidetracking her so that instead of going for him for letting his secretary think they were lovey-dovey with each other—and he was glad that it was so—she was snapping:

'I wasn't *such* an ugly duckling six years ago!'

'Neither you were,' he agreed smoothly, his mouth curving upwards, 'but you'll have to admit you didn't have the—polish then you have now.' And while she coloured at his impertinence, he added coolly, 'Nor if I might be allowed to say,' not waiting for her permission, 'did you have the wherewithal to kit yourself out the way you are now.'

'Kit myself out?' she echoed, suspecting a sting in there somewhere, and sufficient of her temper leaving for her to be wary of the man she knew so little of.

'If memory serves you couldn't in those days afford Givenchy.'

It surprised her momentarily that he should know the name of any designer until she realised he had probably footed some couturier's account on more than one occasion. But she could have done without being reminded of the get-up she had been married in, though she had explained that to him at the time. Then what he was intimating hit her. He thought her clothes were Givenchy models! True, she admired Givenchy more than any other designer, which probably influenced the clothes she made, but ... She stopped as what he was really saying spun through her head. He was saying he didn't think she could afford Givenchy now—that someone else was paying the bill.

'For your information,' she said hotly, anger back with her again, 'no one pays for my clothes but me. For your further information, I am well qualified to make them myself.'

His right eyebrow made a disbelieving arc. Then, 'Ah yes,' he said as though he had just remembered, 'as a matter of fact I checked our marriage certificate last night. You started out as a seamstress.' And suavely, 'May I compliment you on how well I can see you've done in your career.'

Perry didn't thank him. She could well have countered that he too had done well, since he had listed himself as an engineer. But she wasn't here to found a mutual admiration society for work well done.

'Look here, Nash,' she said snappily, and disregarded the signs of interest in his face that here was one female who wasn't a pushover for his charm, 'I didn't come here to discuss the fact that I passed my apprenticeship with honours. I came ...'

'Take a seat, Perry,' he cut in, that stranger of a smile coming to the fore at her look that said she didn't care for the interruption. 'I'm sure our discussion will be far more amicable if you could bring yourself to relax.'

Wondering if he had taken a course in human psychology and learned that one rarely spat fire and brimstone if seated, she took the wooden-backed seat he pulled out for her. Then watched as he pulled his own chair to where he could sit near her, his desk convenient for him to rest a casual arm on.

Taking a deep breath and trying to keep calm, she began again, 'You received my letter, of course?'

'Of course,' he confirmed.

'Before you announced to the press at large that you were hoping for a reconciliation?' She couldn't help the accusing tone and felt like hitting him that he hardly seemed to hear what she said, much less take heed she was accusing him.

'You're not in possession of a telephone yourself?' he enquired casually.

'No.' Her brow furrowed that they were getting nowhere in this interview. 'I told you the phone number in my letter was my landlady's.'

'You're in lodgings?'

What had that got to do with anything? She looked at him then and saw in those shrewd grey eyes that they weren't going to go anywhere with the interview until she answered any questions that presented themselves to him. It irritated her that he had taken charge of the whole affair. But remembering what she wanted the outcome to be, she tried to conceal her impatience and told him more than he had asked to save him thinking up more questions.

'Mrs Foster, my landlady, has arthritis, which means climbing stairs is painful for her. Six years ago she had some alterations made to the upper part of the house, turned it into a sort of a flat, then advertised . . .' She hesitated, expecting sarcasm at the end of it, for all as yet any sarcasm in him had stayed down. 'She advertised for a quiet respectable lady to rent it.'

'So you've been there since our marriage?'

She didn't want to be reminded of those sad days after Ralph's death. 'Almost,' she said quietly.

'Didn't your stepfather object to your moving out?'

His question showed her there was nothing wrong with his memory of what she had told him all that time ago. 'Ralph died a month after we . . .' Her voice petered out.

'And you decided not to stay on at the house you lived in with him?'

'The rent was high there,' she answered without thinking. ·

'You'd just pocketed five thousand pounds and couldn't afford the rent? It must have been high!'

The sarcasm she had known was in him began to show itself. It was something she didn't want, just as she didn't want what she thought his next question would be—What had she done with the money. She forestalled it.

'The five thousand didn't last long.'

'I never thought it would,' he murmured. 'So what do you do for money nowadays? You've never approached me for a penny more, I'll grant you that, but . . .'

'I've never come to you for money because I'm not interested in your money,' she said crossly, and forced herself to calm down as she added, 'I work for every penny I get.'

'Which isn't much and leaves you with very little over,' he surmised, but there was no harshness there, only charm as he said it. He even offered her that smile she could have done with a glimpse of six years ago.

Perhaps it was the very fact that the aggression she had seen in him then, although it must still be there for him to have got where he had, was so totally lacking in the interview that she began to think if she lost her own aggression she might well leave his office with everything just as she wanted it. Her natural self suddenly started to come through, and she smiled back at him, her forehead clear and untroubled beneath her smart hat, her lips curving warmly, her eyes without hostility as she answered:

'I'm paid quite well, actually,' and, a grin tumbling

out, 'but I can't say I'm not grateful to see the end of each month.'

Nash appeared to like it when she relaxed with him, for there were traces of a smile still in his eyes as he studied her sweetly curving mouth. Then his eyes fell to her hands resting quietly in her lap where before they had been fidgeting with the brown leather of her gloves.

'You don't wear your wedding ring,' he remarked easily.

'I dropped it in the river,' she told him openly.

'Recently?'

'Oh no—a couple of hours after the ceremony,' she said, which she thought brought them nicely, and without heat, round to the reason why she was here.

'I can't pretend to understand why you said what you did to the press yesterday,' she said lightly, 'but I really should like to be free, Nash.'

She watched him; his smile had disappeared some moments before, but there had been a smile in his eyes, or so she thought. But as she watched, that smile froze over, and her heart plummeted even before he asked coldly:

'Just what are you up to?' Gone was his casual attitude. Nothing friendly about him now. Aggression she had hoped he would keep hidden not very far from the surface, she was sure.

'What do you mean?' Keep calm, Perry, she tried telling herself, knowing that if her anger grew, met his aggression head on, all hell might break loose.

'Exactly what I say. If you wanted to divorce me there's nothing in the laws of this country to stop you. We've been apart for six years. The marriage hasn't been consummated. Those are just two causes you could use for our marriage being declared void.'

Badly wanting to swallow, Perry didn't dare. Nash would spot it for sure, would know she was nervous and not being totally straightforward as he already suspected.

'I didn't know how you would feel if it leaked into the

papers,' she lied, and tried to lead him, 'I thought you might want a quiet divorce somewhere,' only to find as he gave a harsh unamused laugh, that rankled, that he had seen straight through her lie, straight through her.

'So that's it,' he said triumphantly. 'At first I thought it was a fat alimony settlement you were after. The limited resources you've just told me you possess backed that up.' So that had been the reason for his question of what did she do for money nowadays, she thought, growing angry despite the inner voice that warned her to keep quiet. 'But it isn't that, is it?'

'No, it isn't,' she came back sharply. 'I want nothing from you but my freedom.'

With sparking green eyes she saw Nash looking at her thoughtfully as he registered her swift denial that it was his money she was after. 'There was a doubt in my mind it was money you wanted,' he let her into his thoughts. 'That's why I agreed to see you. It occurred to me you would have made your play long before this had a gold-lined settlement been what you were after.'

'I've just told you,' Perry stormed, getting to her feet in her agitation, 'I want nothing from you.'

Nash pushed his chair away and stood towering over her, tall, broad-shouldered and dark in his immaculate suit, his grey eyes hard, giving her face the closest scrutiny she had ever had to endure. Then when her agitation was threatening to get out of hand, he said calmly:

'I believe you. I believe you want nothing from me but one thing.'

Sorely needing to swallow again as grey eyes pinned, refused to let her look away, she was stunned when without fuss he brought out what his intelligence had told him; the reason she had written to him instead of getting on with it as was her right.

'The only thing you want from me Perry, am I not right, is a *quiet* divorce?'

Shaken, she stared at him. Then as it came to her that

she had been the biggest sort of fool to just write her note and expect Nash to agree without question, hope rose that even not knowing the reason he might yet do as she asked. True, he had let it be known he was married, but surely it still wasn't impossible for a man like him to arrange a quiet divorce?

'Oh, all right,' she said, dragging her eyes away from his hypnotic hold at last. 'You've guessed accurately, of course.' Her mouth firmed at having to confess her lie. 'I apologise for not being straight. But—but it's important to me that we're divorced without it getting into the papers.'

'Why?' he asked shortly. And never, she thought, had any one man made her swing from wanting to be pleasant, on the surface at any rate, to sudden infuriated anger.

'Because—because—oh, if you must know,' she said, angry that he wanted it all when he could so easily have said 'Certainly, leave it to me', 'I want to marry someone else.'

She knew from the way his brows rose that he hadn't been expecting that. And it did nothing for her anger that it clearly hadn't dawned on him that some man some-where might find her attractive enough to fall in love with.

'It's urgent,' she added, revealing all the cards in her hand in one go, ready then to tell him everything if only he would agree. 'Please, Nash,' she said, ready to beg as she visualised her next date with Trevor and her no further forward, still tied with no chance of getting free without his mother reading it in large print in every newspaper. 'I have to be free as soon as possible.'

Already hating herself for so far having forgotten her pride, be ready to beg, she felt her anger go wildly out of control that Nash appeared to look insolently down his nose at her before bringing out the accusation:

'You're pregnant.'

And that was the final frustration in her dealings with him and getting nowhere, that he could so insolently stand there and try to besmirch her character. It was more than she could take. Blistering fury broke at what his clear-thinking brain had summed up; that for the sake of her unborn child it was urgent that she was free of him and married to the child's father without delay, and her hand went whipping through the air. It was the crack that echoed back, notwithstanding the fierce way she was hauled into his arms, that made her realise she had hit him.

'You . . .' he ground out.

But whatever offering he was about to abuse her with, it never got uttered. For enraged grey eyes met furious green eyes, and suddenly the first natural smile she had ever seen on Nash was breaking.

'Was that slap because I hit on the truth, or because you took exception to my remark?' he asked, rage disappearing the longer he looked into her face.

'B-because . . .' Perry tried, growing confused that he still held her, through the pain of his grip mesmerised by the warmth she saw ousting the anger in him. She cleared her throat. 'I'm not pregnant,' she managed to get out.

'Do you know you're the first woman ever to strike me?' The remark was almost conversational.

Wanting to say a sarcastic, he must be pretty nimble on his feet then, she found herself saying, 'If it's any consolation, you're the first man I ever hit.' Then, pulling in vain to get free, she found the acid that a few moments ago had been lost to her. 'Though if what I've read about you is true, you're more used to—to women fawning all over you.'

Unabashed, Nash sighed, 'What it is to be popular!' Then before she could know what he was about, he had pulled her closer. And while her disquieted mind was saying this couldn't be happening, not to her, any of it, his mouth was over hers, and he was kissing her in a way that had her thinking temporarily suspended.

How long the kiss lasted, she couldn't have said. All she knew was that she found it shattering loving Trevor as she did that she didn't in any way feel violated by it. It was thoughts of Trevor trying to get through her subconscious that had her pulling away.

'I didn't come here to—to participate in—in that sort of thing,' she said when Nash dropped his arms to his sides. Putting some space between them, she had to make her voice angry when there was only confusion inside. 'And I'll . . .'

'I never did get to kiss my bride at the start of the marriage,' he chopped her off smoothly, his look sardonic.

'Well, you have no right . . .' she began. Then what he might really be saying righted the confusion in her. Or maybe it was because she felt more the girl she knew she was without those strong arms holding her. At any rate all her hopes were to the front as eagerly she asked, 'Does that mean you—er—kissed me just now because you're agreeing the marriage is over?'

Hope dimmed as a smile she didn't believe in was added to his sardonic look. 'You don't think I owed you something for the slap you just dished out?' he drawled.

'Oh, be fair,' Perry countered, starting to get uptight again. 'How did you expect me to take an accusation like the one you made?'

'Saints preserve us,' he muttered, 'you'll be trotting out next "I'm a good girl, I am".' For the oddest unknown reason she felt her lips wanting to twitch at his mimicry of Eliza Dolittle. Controlling them, she stared stonily, unanswering, at the virile-looking man she had married. 'Very well,' he continued, seeing she wasn't going to rise, 'you've asked me to be fair—so I will be.'

'You will?' Hope was there again, so she just had to let go and smile at him.

Nash was smiling too, pleasantly—too pleasantly, she realised belatedly as calmly he told her, 'As soon as you hand over the sum of five thousand pounds I shall straight away take action to give you your freedom—er—quietly.'

'Five thousand?' she gasped. 'But . . .'

'You're astonished I'm not asking for a penny interest, I can see that,' he sliced urbanely through her stupefied amazement. And while she was still gasping, he added loftily, 'Please don't thank me. I consider you did me a great favour six years ago. In all fairness the least I can do is waive the interest.'

'But . . .' Perry was reeling under what he had just said. 'You—we . . .' and pulling herself together, 'That money never was a loan. You gave it me in exchange for me marrying you.'

'Exactly.' He was smiling no longer, sincerely or insincerely. 'I paid you to marry me. Divorce was never mentioned.'

'But . . .'

'Well, was it?' he challenged.

'No, but . . .'

'There are no buts about it, Perry my dear. It suits me very well to be married and to stay married. Though since you've decided you want to back out of our business arrangement, want, urgently, to be free so you can marry someone else, I'm willing, as I said, to go against a situation that suits me perfectly well and release you from our bargain.'

'For five thousand pounds,' she put in woodenly.

'What sort of business man would I be if I let every contract I made be broken without being compensated?'

Perry espied the devilish light in his eyes, recalled how at the very beginning of this conversation she had as good as told him she lived from month to month for all she was well paid, and saw then that this was the real reason for his questioning and had nothing at all to do with him

thinking she was after his money. He had told her he
thought that had it been his money she was after she would
have made her play before this. Innocently, she had
dropped word after word into his hands for him to make
bullets of and fire back at her when he was ready. And as
she thought about it, Perry grew more furious than she
could ever remember being in her life before.

'You swine!' she muttered between clenched teeth. 'You
utter coldhearted, merciless swine!' His eyebrows rose a
fraction at the unconcealed fury in her, her flashing green
eyes telling any witness she was boiling. 'Five thousand
pounds is neither here nor there to you. But you know
damn well I'd be hard put to find five hundred, let alone
five thousand. I as good as told you that myself, didn't I?'

'Perhaps you were a little indiscreet,' Nash commented,
seeming to be thoroughly enjoying the five feet seven fire-
brand standing in front of him blazing away.

'Indiscreet!' Her voice rose, all previous attempts to
keep Karen Taylor from knowing any of their discussion
forgotten in her fury. 'You deliberately led me into telling
you about my finances!' And at his look that said taking
candy from a baby couldn't have been easier, she lost
control completely, and forgetful too how quickly Nash
had moved the last time she had physically set about him,
she aimed a crack at his shin that would have crippled
him for the rest of the day had it connected. Only it
didn't.

With lightning speed he moved out of the way. And
since she was off balance he had not the slightest trouble
in picking her up and plonking her down heavily on his
desk.

The feeling of looking ridiculous sitting there with her
legs dangling in no way helped to quieten her fury.

'Let go of me!' she yelled, when, taking no chances,
Nash held her there.

'Like hell I will,' he retorted, hanging on to her grimly
as she tried to wriggle free.

Then to her amazement, he threw back his head and laughed. It was a deep and natural sound and so entirely unexpected Perry forgot her anger and just sat and stared at him.

'Forgive me,' he said after a moment, and a more unrepentant plea for forgiveness she had never heard.

'Why should I?' she asked belligerently.

'Perhaps I'll tell you the next time we meet,' he suggested, taking his restraining hold from her.

Her anger resurfaced as she slid down from her undignified perch. 'There'll be no next time,' she said tautly, and saw his eyes narrow briefly before, his face serious, though his manner more confident than ever, he said softly:

'So you intend to set the divorce ball rolling without my help—regardless of all the accompanying ballyhoo?'

Inwardly defeated, Perry lifted her elegantly clad head proudly. 'Go to hell, Nash Devereux!' she snapped, and wished with all her heart that she had succeeded in temporarily crippling him as his laughter followed her out of the door.

She had found her interview with Nash Devereux draining. He was better looking than she had remembered, and newsprint didn't do him full justice, but that hardness that had been in him six years ago was still there.

Asking for his money back before he'd do the decent thing and quietly divorce her, she fumed, as she made her way home. Where did he think she was going to find five thousand pounds?

Still indignant at the easy way he had ruined her sophisticated image by hoisting her on to his desk, she knew she had been right to leave his office. Had she stayed she just knew he would have managed to make her feel an even bigger fool than he had already made her feel.

Unfeeling brute that he was, business was the only thing that concerned him. That he considered her part and parcel of a business deal made six years ago was obvious.

Inwardly Perry cringed at the way she had been so open with him about the state of her finances. Talk about handing him ammunition on a plate! And why, oh, why hadn't she belted him again after he had kissed her? Like a lamb she had stood in his arms for a full five seconds, mesmerised by the feel of those experienced lips on hers.

Too emotionally mixed up to think of going into work that afternoon—they weren't expecting her anyway—she changed into jeans and sweater and let her hair down about her shoulders. Then she spent the rest of the day until six o'clock with tidying her flat, doing some washing, while at the same time railing angrily against Nash Devereux and wondering what on earth did she do now.

At six a knock on her door showed Mrs Foster had opened the front door to Trevor and sent him up, explaining as he entered her sitting room that he had rung her place of work.

'The girl on the switchboard said you had an appointment and had left,' he said, letting her know the telephonist's ears were not limited to telephone monitoring, 'but I didn't believe her because you hadn't said anything to me about it. So I told her to put me through to Madge.' Feeling queasy inside that the time had come when she had to explain what her appointment was all about, Perry cleared her throat as he continued, 'Madge told me you had an upset stomach and had gone home. I knew you didn't have an appointment. How are you feeling now, darling?'

'Er—Trevor,' she began, and as the moment arrived, her upset stomach was no figment of Madge's imagination, not now anyway.

'You're very pale,' said Trevor before her full courage came to her. And in sudden alarm, 'You're not going to be sick, are you?'

'No, I'm not going to be sick,' she said to his patent relief. 'I . . .' the words to tell him stuck.

'Good, good.' Visibly he brightened, and suggested that since by the look of her she was still far from well it might be an idea if she sat down.

He sat with her on the settee, his hand holding hers, while she sought desperately for just the right words to tell him what couldn't be kept from him any longer.

'It came to me while I was driving here,' Trevor was saying before anything very tactful had come to her in the way of dressing up what she had to tell him, 'that you really shouldn't be living here all on your own, not with your fragile constitution.'

'Fragile constitution!' She was as strong as a horse, always full of energy. But his interpretation of her delicate colouring had astounded her into forgetting for the moment what had made her paler than usual.

'You seldom have any colour in your cheeks,' he pointed out in reply to her startled exclamation, apparently unaware of the many young women who would give their eye teeth to have the finely tinted skin that went so well with her hair and eyes. 'And with Madge saying how poorly you were this morning, how you should have someone to look after you—well, it came to me as I was coming along that I might be being a bit—well, just a shade too careful in wanting to be sure before I ask you to marry me.'

'Oh!' Perry was at a loss to know what else to say as she wondered at Madge's motherly instincts coming to ripeness at precisely this time.

'Perhaps I've been so long in insurance that I wanted the policy to be sound before I took it out,' said Trevor, and didn't see that she winced at his choice of words if this was supposed to be a romantic moment. 'Anyway, darling,' he added, giving her hand a squeeze, 'I think we should get married.'

'Trevor, I . . .'

'You do want to marry me, don't you?' He looked put

out already that the look of delight that should have been on her face wasn't there.

'Yes, yes, of course,' she said quickly. 'It's just that I . . .' she had been going to say 'have something to tell you first', but before she could finish, he finished it for her:

'It's just that with your upset stomach you're not up to showing the happiness you feel.' And before she could contradict him, 'If you're better tomorrow we'll go out and celebrate, shall we?'

'Trevor, I must . . .'

'The only "must" you have, darling, is to go to bed early. Have an early night, I want you in tip-top form by tomorrow. Oh, damn!' clearly he had just remembered something. 'I forgot, I'm taking Mother to visit Aunt Hetty for the weekend, you remember I told you about it. We won't be back until late Sunday.' He squeezed her hand again. 'Never mind, we'll have our celebration on Monday night.'

Perry's emotions had been frayed before Trevor arrived. When very shortly afterwards he went, staying only to display his thoughtfulness in presenting her with the evening paper he knew she enjoyed but would be too poorly to go and collect herself, her emotions were positively shredded.

She just couldn't believe she had actually agreed to marry him without first telling him about Nash Devereux! But that pleased expression on his face, after he'd told her he wouldn't kiss her in case he got her germs. told her she had.

Oh lord, she groaned wearily, picking up the evening paper with a listless hand in the hope of immersing herself in print and so get away for a short while from the thoughts that were going to nag at her all night. She opened the paper, saw one large headline, and her groan that time was one filled with anguish.

'WHO IS THE MYSTERIOUS MRS DEVEREUX?'

the headline read. Hardly daring to read on, she found a temporary reprieve in the start of the smaller print to read, 'After revealing yesterday that he has a wife, that is all Nash Devereux is revealing. Our reporter today . . .'

Perry let the paper drop. Nash still wasn't saying—but for how long would he keep her name to himself?

CHAPTER FIVE

THE fact that she had spent a depressed and worrying weekend must have been showing, Perry thought when she presented herself at work on Monday and saw Madge, who had arrived at the same time, looking at her closely.

'How's the tummy upset?' she enquired, her way of saying that regardless of the invention, Perry didn't look up to par.

'Thanks, Madge,' said Perry, knowing Madge would take from that her thanks for covering for her and also that she didn't want to discuss anything to do with Friday.

'Any time,' Madge replied. Then with a, 'Heads down time,' she prepared to start work.

The trouble with this job, Perry thought, as she threaded a needle, was that it gave one plenty of time to think. And she had done more than enough chasing the same theme on Saturday and Sunday when a feeling of thoroughly disliking Nash Devereux had made itself felt. It was all his fault, she had thought time and time again, that the celebratory evening with Trevor she should have been eagerly looking forward to held nothing for her but guilt at the secret that was between them.

She should be happy and excited, she thought, recalling the agony of her thoughts over the weekend, that soon she would be celebrating her engagement with the man she loved. For it had come to her, in long wakeful hours, that by not rejecting Trevor's proposal she must now be engaged to him.

Unconsciously she sighed, her sigh heard by Madge, who looked up, wanting to help with whatever was troubling her, but unable to unless Perry confided in her.

Oh, where was she to get five thousand pounds from? Perry wondered agitatedly. Even if Trevor had got five thousand she couldn't ask or accept it from him. She had taken money from one man once, admittedly not for herself, and look where it had got her! Not that there would be any trouble with Trevor if he gave her the five thousand she so badly needed, she mentally defended him, it was just her—she just couldn't ask him.

Madge repeated the same words Trevor had said to her on Friday as they were leaving at the end of the day. 'I should have an early night if I were you,' she advised.

Perry blamed Nash entirely that the spontaneous 'Not tonight, tonight Trevor and I are celebrating our engagement' was never made.

'I will,' she promised instead, and went home so fed up with herself she knew she had reached the end of the road. When Trevor called, *before* they went out she would invite him in, would tell him everything. She loved him, she couldn't bear the thought of losing him, but if after what she had told him he no longer wanted to take her out, then she would have to accept that. But tell him she was going to; she couldn't go on like this one minute more than she had to.

But barely had she closed the door of her sitting room after stopping at Mrs Foster's to leave the small bits of shopping she had picked up for her in her lunch hour than her landlady was calling her down to the telephone.

Trevor, she thought, hurrying down the stairs so as not to keep him waiting, smiling her thanks to Mrs Foster as she limped into the kitchen so she could take her call in private.

But it wasn't Trevor, and Perry's dislike of Nash Devereux rose to the top as she heard his voice, easy, supremely self-assured and enquiring if she'd just got in from work. If he had telephoned just to enquire jibingly if she had the five thousand for him yet, then regardless of the damage to Mrs Foster's phone, Perry was certain she would be sending the instrument crashing down with a force that would shatter it.

'As a matter of fact, yes,' she replied as evenly as she could.

'Good,' was her answer. 'I wanted to catch you before you began cooking your evening meal.' And while her brain was trying to make sense of that remark, he was adding,

'Have dinner with me.'

Of all the nerve! Who *did* he think he was? Not only had he seemed to have forgotten she had stormed out of his office on Friday, but his voice sounded fully confident she wouldn't refuse. Just as though she was one of his little dillies who went into ecstasies at the mere sound of his voice, ready to drop anything they were doing at the merest hint he might like to take them to dinner, she fumed:

'The kindness of your invitation overwhelms me, Mr Devereux,' sweetness fairly dripped before anger soured it and had her snapping, 'I'd sooner jump fully clothed in the Thames than dine with you!'

The sound of genuine laughter in her ear, telling her that instead of offending him she had managed only to amuse him, arrested her when she would have slammed the phone down. She hesitated a moment too long and heard his voice again, still confident damn him:

'We never did get down to seriously discussing our divorce, did we?'

He had her hooked and he knew it, Perry seethed. But she was still hanging on to the phone.

'I thought we had,' she said stubbornly, not allowing hope to rise—she had been fooled before.

'You didn't think I was serious when I asked you to return the money, did you?'

'Of course I did.' Hope was there despite what her

brain was telling her, that this was some game he was playing purely for his own amusement. 'You meant me to think you were serious.' She waited, hoping he would insert something, but when it was all silent his end, she just had to add, 'Are you now saying that you weren't— that you were just—just baiting me?'

'I think,' he spoke at last, and she didn't like at all that there was a mocking note in his voice when he said, 'it really is a case of "my wife doesn't understand me".'

'I'm not your . . .' She stopped. For all Mrs Foster wasn't in sight she might well overhear what she was saying.

'I have a paper that proves it,' said Nash.

'Unfortunately so do I,' Perry said frigidly—then became all hot and bothered that he would think it mattered that much to her that she had sent for such a document. 'A copy, anyway,' she qualified. 'I couldn't believe it had all happened afterwards—so,' her voice tailed off lamely, 'I sent for a copy.'

'Wasn't the five thousand proof enough?' he queried, the mocking note gone as talk of the money she had taken hardened something in him.

It stiffened something in Perry too, or maybe it was just his altered tone. 'Why should it matter to you? You're well used to girls like me,' she jibed, regardless that he might find the remark painful. And anyway, he had a hide as thick as an elephant's, so why should she bother?

'You're wrong there,' he corrected. 'You're a new type to me. While I admit that something in your adolescence had you selling yourself to a perfect stranger, you've grown into a very self-respecting young woman, who against my experience is at this moment, I imagine, hating to be reminded of what avarice had you doing at eighteen.'

For a moment, a glow suffusing her that Nash had every confidence she was no longer some money-hungry female, Perry had the strangest urge to tell him she never had been. Then she saw that was what he wanted. By using the word avarice he was trying to prick her into explaining why she had sold herself to him the way she had, just as though for him it didn't add up. And even though Ralph had been dead for so long, loyalty to him would have had her holding her tongue without the stubbornness in her that said she was explaining nothing to Nash Devereux.

'It would be a poor sort of individual who never regretted any of the things they'd done in the past,' she trotted out instead.

A pause, then he was agreeing, 'It would indeed,' and then as though he was in a hurry and considered he had already spent too long in idle conversation, 'So do we dine together tonight to discuss righting a wrong committed six years ago or not?'

About to tell him no, Perry came up against the better of her two options. Either she had to tell Trevor tonight or, which would be preferable, another night when she might be able to tell him Nash had agreed to a quiet divorce somewhere.

'Where shall I meet you?' The decision was made, the words out, panic at the thought of losing Trevor making a coward of her.

'I'm the old-fashioned kind,' she was informed, mockery deliberately there this time just to annoy her, she thought, growing angry. 'I always call to pick up my dates.'

'It's not a date,' she snapped, and did then what had threatened a few times during their conversation—she banged the phone down. Then she stood there idiotically looking at it, only then wondering if Nash would think from her parting remark that she had declined to go out with him after all.

'Cup of tea, Perry, I've just made a pot?'

Mrs Foster coming out of her kitchen had her turning. 'Er—no, thanks, Mrs Foster. I'm—er—going out tonight, so I'd better do something about getting ready.'

She was at the door before thought of the disaster that could happen smote her. Oh, lord! What if Nash discounted her last remark and did call for her? What if he arrived on the doorstep at the same time as Trevor? Panic threatening to have her going under had her turning back to Mrs Foster.

'Could I use the phone to make a call?' she asked quickly, adding more slowly, 'I've just remembered something.'

'Of course, dear, you know you don't have to ask. I'll leave you to it. You can let yourself out.'

Her insides churning, Perry dialled Trevor's number. Hating what she was about to do, she just couldn't face the alternative of what would happen if both men arrived at the same time. Dreadful visions filled her mind of Nash and Trevor on the doorstep, Nash calmly introducing himself as her husband.

'Trevor—me,' she said on a gulp when he answered the phone—and had to suffer great pangs of conscience when he enquired how she was, in having to pretend her fictitious tummy bug hadn't cleared up.

'I don't think I would be very good company tonight,' she added.

'Well, you certainly won't do full justice to the meal I thought we'd have,' he agreed. 'It would be a shame to waste good money on something you're not going to eat.'

That Trevor was obviously afraid of catching her germs by instead of suggesting he would come round and sit with her anyway, said he would ring tomorrow to see how she was, might have had her wondering about the depth of his love. But she was so heartily glad the possibility of him bumping into Nash had been eliminated, it was all she could think about.

That was until she was back upstairs, and then the only thought that filled her mind was, did she have a date with Nash Devereux or didn't she?

Just in case, she had a quick bath, and recalling that she had looked as near the height of elegance as she was likely to get when she had seen him Friday, she rummaged through her wardrobe in an endeavour to find something that would keep up her image.

She found it in a brown velvet classically cut dress Trevor had never liked. It made her appear too remote, he had said, its slim-fitting line making her appear tall, regal, and not his Perry at all. Which was funny, because it always felt so right on, she thought, dressing her hair in the way she had worn it on Friday.

At eight she had been ready ten minutes. At ten past eight she decided it had been a wasted effort and she might as well settle her rumbling tummy with some beans on toast. Nash wasn't coming, she knew he wasn't, she thought at twenty past eight, starving hungry. When the front door bell went at half past eight, so did her appetite.

Opening her door, she heard voices in the hall below, realised Mrs Foster must have been in the hall when the bell went, and quickly closed it again. The insecurity of her late teens was back with her. She didn't want Nash telling Mrs Foster who he was, and for the same reason she couldn't go down and introduce the two of them.

She had her door open again within seconds of Nash knocking on it and for a moment could do nothing but stand looking at him. Dressed in a dinner jacket, she thought, he looked almost handsome. Then she saw from the way he was looking at her, that he too seemed to appreciate what he saw.

'Do I get to come in?' he hinted when she had made no move to step back.

'Sorry.' Her voice and movement back into the room were automatic. Then, spinning round, 'You didn't tell Mrs Foster who you are? I mean, that we're . . .'

'Ashamed of me, Perry?' he mocked, his eyes glinting with humour.

'No, of course not,' she said before she read the devilment in his eyes.

'Nor am I ashamed of you,' he told her, a suggestion of a smile coming to a mouth that was at once firm, yet hinted at sensuality. 'Nor,' he added, his eyes admiring, 'would any man be. I thought yesterday that you'd turned out to be quite something, but the only word that fits you tonight, is stunning.'

Perry cleared her throat. 'Yes, well,' she said, unable to deny she found his practised charm agreeable, but sternly trying to remind herself he had probably trotted out that self-same remark times without number, 'since the only reason we're meeting tonight is to revolve a business matter, whether you think I look stunning or as plain as a pikestaff doesn't come into it, does it?'

For answer, the suggestion of a smile that had been on his mouth broke into a very decided grin, and Perry had the very definite feeling that had she been as plain as a pikestaff she might well have been feeding off beans on toast.

Nash took her to a very exclusive gentlemen's club of which he was a member. 'Apropos not being ashamed of each other, I thought you might prefer to dine where members of the press fraternity will not be allowed in with their cameras,' he explained, and received from her a natural smile for his thoughtfulness.

Though her smile was nowhere to be seen when, confused by the choice of menu, she said she would have the same as him, Nash told the punctilious head waiter:

'My wife will have the boeuf bourguignon, Thomas, so will I.'

'How *could* you!' she hissed the moment the waiter was out of earshot. And when Nash looked as though he didn't have a clue what she was talking about, 'You didn't have to tell him I was your wife.'

'It's more than Thomas's job is worth to indulge in

gossip,' Nash told her, entirely unconcerned that she looked furious, reminding her when she needed no reminding, and managing to seem surprised that she had forgotten, 'And you *are* my wife, aren't you?'

'Not for much longer, if I have my way,' she fumed.

'Relax, Perry my dear,' said Nash blandly. 'We have plenty of time in which to discuss the ending of what for me has been a blissful six years of married life.'

He'd done it again! His dry humour had made her want to laugh. Though she quickly sobered, her lips refusing to twitch at his intimation that six years without her was all a man could ask for. And that annoyed her too, that following on from wanting to laugh, she should feel— piqued? It was ridiculous. Good heavens! Those six years, apart from losing Ralph, had been quite blissful for her too, hadn't they?

'There's no need for your life to be any less blissful now than it was before,' she began. 'As soon as . . .' only to be stopped by Nash briefly touching her hand.

'I refuse to have our digestions ruined by discussing something that will only take a few minutes and can well wait until after we've eaten,' he said decisively. And at her questioning look, 'You being you, Perry, I don't for a minute doubt we'd be able to have a straightforward discussion on the matter without you becoming—er— heated.'

Reminiscently he rubbed the side of his face, deliberately provoking the memory that the last time they had discussed the subject, she had hit him. And when it wasn't funny at all, she had the hardest work in the world to hold down a gurgle of laughter.

'Tell me about yourself, Perry Bethia Grainger,' he said after a moment. 'Just when did the—casually-dressed female I married emerge from her chrysalis?'

Loath to talk about herself—it went without saying that he had led a far more exciting life—she found Nash a master in drawing people out. So much so snippets of her life before that fateful meeting with him that day came, hesitatingly at first, from her.

'So you never knew your father?' Nash inserted when she had told him of her father's death when she was a baby, and her mother's death when she was seventeen.

'No,' she replied, and remembering the way he had spoken of his father six years ago and recalling the feeling she had had then that there must have been a deep love between father and son, she defended, not thinking herself in need of pity if that was what that look in his eyes meant, 'But I didn't miss out on a father's love, if that's what you're thinking.'

The look she had thought pitying went from him, his expression was now mockingly enquiring, just as though, she thought crossly, he was assuming she had taken up with some sugar-daddy as a father replacement figure.

'No?' he queried, his sardonically quirking lips telling her she had read his thoughts correctly.

'No,' she said tightly, only just keeping her anger in check, though not her tongue, as the heat of the moment forced her on. 'My mother married Ralph when I was five. Ralph gave me more love than a lot of girls get from their true father. He . . .'

'I thought you had a hate thing going with him?' Nash interrupted sharply. 'That's the impression you gave me. Or was the family love only from his side?'

As she remembered clearly that she had wanted him to think exactly as he had, the heat went from her. It might be as well to discontinue this topic before it went any farther, she thought, but at that moment the love she had for Ralph chose to rise up, and she could no more deny how dear he had been to her than fly.

'I—yes, I did give you that impression, I know,' she confessed. And even though Ralph had been dead six years her eyes misted over as she choked, 'But he was the dearest man to me. I missed him very much when he died.'

Nash didn't go into why had she let him think what he had, but said, 'That was a month after our marriage, I think you said,' and there was a warm note in his voice that had her thinking he was remembering the love he had felt for his own father and how he had felt at the time of losing him.

And suddenly she found an empathy flowing between them. She raised her eyes, saw her senses had not played her false. The encouraging curve to Nash's mouth, the compassion in his eyes both worked on her sensitivities of the moment, and she found herself telling him:

'I was so mixed up then, confused. Ralph and I were friends as well as step-relatives. Even after my mother's death I hadn't felt so alone. There'd been a lot to arrange as well as the worry of what to do about the house we were living in. I knew I couldn't afford to keep it on,' she said, forgetting entirely that only a month earlier Nash had given her five thousand pounds. But he didn't interrupt to remind her, and she went on, 'I wasn't earning very much then. So I was in a bit of a state in not only knowing I would have to find a flat, leave the house and get rid of a houseful of furniture, but worst of all there would be no Ralph to come home to.'

Whether Nash was touched by her revelation of that awful time she had experienced as a young eighteen-year-old, she didn't stop to wonder. But she knew the empathy she had felt was still there when his hand came across the pristine white tablecloth and rested lightly over hers.

'Confused as you were, you couldn't believe you'd recently stood in front of a registrar and married a stranger?' Perry smiled softly at him, silently amazed that he should understand. She nodded her agreement. 'It was then you sent for a copy of the certificate. You needed to prove to yourself it had really happened, that you weren't going round the bend?'

Nash putting it into words—so exactly on beam, it had a smile coming from her for him and his insight into how she had been at the time.

'Yes,' she agreed quietly. And as he took his hand from hers, her mind grew full of that time in her eighteenth year, and her smile faded as she recalled the money Nash had given her, money she had given to Ralph, dear-dead Ralph. 'I needn't have married you, taken your money at all,' she said bleakly, her thoughts so taken up with Ralph, she was barely aware in that sad moment of her thoughts of what she was saying.

But Nash was aware, and, she realised a moment later, blade-sharp when it came to analysing even half-given information.

'The money was for your stepfather,' he guessed shrewdly, but kept his voice low as though knowing the slightest suggestion of hardness would have her lips sealed.

'I ...' she began—and only then came alive to what conclusions he could draw. Talking about her stepfather as she had been and then referring to the marriage and the money in the same breath ... She shook her head, confirmation of what she had known all along there— Nash Devereux was much too sharp for her.

'Ralph was in debt,' he pressed, a calculating look appearing in his eyes that had her reacting coldly.

'It's all water under the bridge now, isn't it?' she said stiffly, intending to tell him nothing more, heartily wishing she had never told him anything.

'So he was,' Nash prodded, obviously not ready to leave the matter there despite the look on her face that told him he had heard all he was going to from her. 'That's why it was so important for you to have a well-heeled husband,' he went on, all the warmth he had shown her vanishing promptly, ejected by the swift coldness that came to him as he pressed, 'You couldn't think of any other way to get the money to settle his debts, so you opted for a rich husband.'

Perry stayed mute, the line of her mouth stubborn. He could think what the hell he liked, he wasn't getting another word out of her!

He kept his eyes on her as he waited for her reply, the stubborn mulish look in the green eyes that glared back silently saying he would have a long wait. Another second ticked by, then he was biting into her:

'Or was it Ralph's idea that you get yourself a rich husband?' Green eyes sparked dangerously, but she said nothing. 'Did this man you state so confidently loved you as if you were his own—did he love you so well he thought up the bright idea that you sell yourself to . . .'

Something inside her broke to have this swine of a man denigrating the affection she knew her stepfather had for her. 'He did love me,' she blazed, 'he did! He would have been horrified if he'd known how I got the money I gave him.' In her fury she was totally unaware what she had just confirmed as she raged on: 'And for your information, I didn't go to the marriage bureau to find a husband, but because I had an appointment with the woman who ran it—Ralph's sister.'

She saw his eyes narrow as in a flash he had dissected that piece of information. 'You intended asking her for the money?' he questioned rapidly, and while Perry was gasping at the quickness of his brain, she was also reeling that in her fury she had told him as much as she had.

Stubbornness entered her face again. But Nash now had everything he wanted to know. He smiled, a smile she took no pleasure from and didn't believe in either.

'You knew from her locked office that she had no intention of keeping her appointment with you,' he said, neatly tying up any loose ends. 'You knew you wouldn't be getting a penny from her. But as soon as I mentioned the sum I was prepared to pay for a bride without strings, you just had to consider throwing in with me.'

Perry tossed him a look of hearty dislike which bounced

right off him as he smiled that insincere smile and suggested that since she had finished her coffee would she like more.

Startled, she looked down into her empty coffee cup. Her boeuf bourguignon had been delicious, but she had no recollection of eating the next course or emptying her coffee cup.

'No, thank you,' she said woodenly.

'In that case, if you're ready, we'll go.'

'But—but we haven't discussed the divorce yet,' she protested, about to remind him that that was the only reason she had come out with him anyway.

'You're not home yet,' he said before she could add another word.

Perry got to her feet, her face mutinous as Nash took her arm to escort her from the dining room.

'I should like to go straight home,' she said abruptly as he handed her into his sleek car.

'Yours or mine?' was the mocking reply.

'Don't be funny,' she answered cuttingly.

But his remark had unnerved her, and it was with anxious eyes that she watched the direction he steered the car. Just one wrong turn, she thought, and Nash Devereux might yet wind up on the receiving end of his second blow dealt by a woman's hand!

CHAPTER SIX

But Perry found her fears that he intended they should go to his place unfounded. And so fixedly had she been watching the route he was taking that they arrived at her flat with the matter of the divorce still unresolved.

Nash turned off the engine, but she had no intention of moving until the item of conversation he had said would only take a few minutes was satisfactorily agreed on.

'We'll talk in your flat,' he stated with that disgusting self-confidence of his.

'We won't . . .' was as far she got before he was slipping quickly, effortlessly from behind the wheel and was round at her side of the car helping her out.

He really was the limit! she fumed, ready to hit him with something heavy if once in her flat he suggested she gave him coffee.

'Nice place you have here,' he remarked on entering her sitting room for the second time that evening. 'Shall I light the gas fire for you? It's still cold for this time of year, isn't it?'

I'll brain him yet! Perry was thinking as, with anger building up inside, she watched the loose-limbed way he strolled over to her gas fire and put a match to it.

'Now,' he said, that mocking smile doing nothing for her blood pressure, 'shall we sit down and discuss the subject that by the look of you is threatening to have you blowing a gasket?'

It's not the subject, she wanted to retort, it's you. But that he now seemed ready to get down to business had a calming effect on her as she chose to sit down on the settee, keeping a lid tightly shut when her anger would have erupted again when he ignored the easy chair facing her and opted to join her on the settee.

'Why is the divorce suddenly so urgent?' he enquired, coming straight to the point, and adding before she could remind him, 'I know you intend marrying again—but you never did get around to giving me the reason for such haste.'

'I . . .' she began, not wanting to be amused at his mocking reference to the slap he had received for an answer the time before. She controlled her lips that wanted to curve upwards as she wondered what chance she had got of a quiet divorce if she refused to answer him this time. She looked at him and knew from the way he was quietly waiting that she would have to tell him before he would begin to get down to discussing the serious business of the divorce.

'Well—if you must know,' she said, hating him for making her confess, 'Er—Trevor—Trevor doesn't know yet that I've been—that I'm married.'

There was no mockery at all in Nash as his eyes pierced through her. 'Doesn't know . . .'

'I've tried to tell him,' Perry quickly jumped in, pink with guilt and sensing censure with a few unpleasant comments thrown in, 'but—but—well, his mother has such a thing about divorce,' she defended, 'she'll spoil everything between us if she knows.' She grew flustered that what she had said in no way explained why she hadn't told the person it concerned most. She tried again. 'Trevor won't mind when I explain everything to him,' she said, more in hope than in justification. 'It's just that I would rather tell him when it's all over—when I'm free, if you see what I mean.'

Nash was streets ahead of her, she could see that. 'He *has* asked you to marry him?' he asked bluntly.

The question, the look that went with it that said he didn't think much of any girl who would let a man get that far and still nurse the secret she was nursing, had her colour going high again.

'I—well,' she said, trying to vindicate herself even while

knowing she had no defence, 'well, Trevor said he was only thinking about asking me to marry him,' she tried, and saw that Nash, being a man of instant decisions, didn't look to think much of Trevor either since he appeared to be a man who waffled before he made up his mind, and found she was having to defend Trevor as well as herself. 'With his mother so against divorce and . . . and Trevor as well—for himself, that is,' she said. Then, hating to be so much on the defensive, she threw her hands up in an Oh, dammit! gesture.

'This has nothing to do with you and me,' she said agitatedly. 'The other night Trevor asked me to marry him. I didn't mean to say yes without telling him, but I must have done because we were supposed to go out tonight to celebrate. I was definitely going to tell him tonight, but . . .'

'But I rang,' said Nash, his look softening in the face of her obvious agitation. 'So you decided you would see me first and hope to be able to tell the doting Trevor the next time you saw him that at least the divorce was under way?'

Perry saw his smile was genuine this time. 'Oh, Nash,' she sighed, not meaning to sound so utterly fed up as she did, 'I've been in such a panic!'

The smile disappeared from his mouth, but his eyes were kind as he studied her sad face. 'Come here,' he said softly.

Uncertain, the insecurity in her found comfort when he put an arm around her and she felt the side of her face against his shoulder. She sighed and needed the solidness of a hard shoulder at that moment.

'Poor little Perry,' he murmured.

'I've been so worried, so miserable,' she confessed. 'I rang your office nearly two weeks ago and was told you'd that day left for the States, so I wrote that night and rushed home every day to see if there was any answer in the post.'

'And panicked again when you saw in the paper that I was hoping to be reconciled with my wife,' he said softly in her ear, his other hand coming to stroke the side of her face, causing alarm bells to give the faintest suggestion of a tinkle. 'I'll bet you nearly fell off your bike when you opened up the paper,' he teased gently, his breath warm on her ear, his teasing quieting any alarms as her mouth winged upwards.

'Why did you do it, Nash? I mean, only your solicitor and Lydia knew you were married anyway, didn't they?' She tried to move out of his arm, but his hold was firm. But she didn't panic that he wasn't letting her go. Nash wasn't the sort to attempt rape, and she could soon tell him to cut it out if he tried any funny business. 'Why *did* you suddenly announce it to the world?' she questioned.

She felt him shrug, before he answered casually, 'A culmination of reasons, possibly. I'd just stepped from a plane, tired after working flat out, not wanting to be met by the press or—anyone.' Did that mean that the lovely Elvira Newman pictured—clinging to him was on her way out? It sounded very much like it, though there was no time for her to speculate further, for he was going on, 'But since I wanted to look in on the office I arranged to meet the press there hoping to call it a day afterwards. At my office, tired like I said, probably feeling anti-climax now that a tough assignment had been satisfactorily completed after hard days that went on into the nights, and jaded most likely, I flipped through my mail and came across one letter marked "Strictly Private and Confidential".'

'Mine,' she put in needlessly.

'Private and confidential correspondence I deal with regularly,' Nash told her. 'It was the "Strictly" that had me opening it.'

'Before you saw the press?'

She felt the muscles of his face move against hers, realised there must be a grin on his face, and felt her heart go thump as she realised too that his face was warm against

hers, cheek to cheek! And she hadn't felt him move!
Quickly she moved her face away, turning to see his satisfied smile, a glimmer of pure reminiscent devilment in his
eyes.

'Your letter intrigued me—had tiredness leaving as I
read what you'd written.'

'I wouldn't have thought the few lines I wrote were all
that stimulating,' said Perry, trying desperately to recall
word for word what she had finally penned, and wishing
too late that she had made a copy.

'It was what you didn't write I found fascinating,' Nash
informed her. 'It didn't matter to me who knew I was
married—but it didn't take any master-mind to read that
it did to you.'

'So you told the press you were hoping for a reconciliation—just to frighten the life out of me,' she said, catching
on quickly.

'That wasn't my intention,' he denied. 'Though I did
think you had a shake-up coming.'

'Why what had I done?' she asked aggressively. 'It
wasn't as though I was like your other women, was it—
I didn't want anything from you but . . .'

'But your freedom,' he ended, then fully enlightened
her. 'It was your dishonesty that had me doing what I
did.'

'Dishonesty?'

'You've just revealed that you remember the way I
regard women, how other women appear to me. You must
have known I didn't want a divorce, that the marriage
didn't bother me, that if it had I would have done
something about it long ago. Yet you didn't have that
much honesty to give me your real reason for wanting a
divorce—"if it's all right with you" you wrote, "I should
like to be free. Would you let me know as soon as possible
if you are agreeable to a divorce?" Well, I wasn't, so I
took the least bothersome way to tell you I wasn't.'

'Thanks for nothing!' snapped Perry, ready to fly at

him. Then remembering something had to ask, 'Though I suppose I should thank you that you kept my name out of the paper—why did you, by the way?'

'Blame it on my soft old heart,' said the man who must, she thought, have the hardest heart of any man she had ever met, the very devil dancing in his eyes. 'You certainly won't credit me with any gentlemanly instinct for not wanting the eighteen-year-old I remembered, regardless of the dishonesty she was practising, to receive some of the type of hounding by the press I've suffered in my day.'

'I didn't mean to be dishonest,' she told him, her anger going at his consideration in keeping her name to himself, forgetful for the moment, that he would have saved her a lot more nagging worry had he not said anything to the press at all. 'I've told you I was in a panic, worried about Trevor, his mother.'

'I'll forgive you.' said Nash magnanimously, 'just as you forgave me for laughing in my office on Friday when I had you perched on my desk.'

'Why did you?' she asked, taken out of her stride, and remembering then that he had suggested he might tell her the next time he saw her. Remembering too that she had said then that there would be no next time—did he always get his own way?

'Call it relief from utter boredom.' The corners of his mouth curved upwards and, finding it infectious, Perry had the hardest work in keeping her mouth from following suit as he explained, 'I've already told you you're a new type to me. Perhaps I've dated too many of the same kind of woman, but there you were, not the least interested in me or my pocket. Spitting fire and ready to bash my head in—and do you know something, Perry?' his voice softened, a seductive quality entering. 'Beautiful as you are, like other women of my acquaintance, I knew then I could never be bored with you around.'

'I . . .' she began, and realising full well that this sort of talk was getting nothing settled in the way of the divorce, felt herself becoming spellbound by the seductive way he was speaking. 'I . . . I think,' she said, trying to shake free of the hypnotic hold she seemed to be in, 'I think we ought—should . . .'

'Do you want to know what I think?' Nash asked softly, his look going from her eyes to her mouth.

'No,' came from her, sounding nowhere near as firm as it was meant to. Then something inside her was disobeying what her brain was telling her to do, to get up from the settee and sit somewhere else as his hand came to her face, his fingers stroking her fine skin. 'Wh-what do you think?' she found herself asking huskily.

He smiled, and if there was triumph lurking in that smile at the transfixed look of her, the husky note in her voice, then she missed it as she swallowed and looked down.

'I think,' he murmured, 'that the least you owe me for keeping your name out of the papers is—a kiss.'

'I—you kissed me on Friday,' she reminded him, her heart going crazy, all thought of Trevor forgotten. Never had she realised one could be seduced with so much ease; she barely realised it now.

'Exactly. It was I who did the kissing.'

Getting to know Nash as she was, Perry knew then that nothing further was going to be discussed until she had complied with his request. Though what they had to discuss was starting to grow dimmer and dimmer in her mind.

'Very well,' she said, and, determined to treat the matter lightly, good sense demanded it, 'Pucker up!'

Nash stayed still, making no move to meet her half way as she leaned forward ready to salute his mouth briefly with hers. She hesitated a few inches away from him, looked straight into warm grey eyes that were so near, and a choking sensation hitting her dropped her eyes to that equally warm waiting mouth.

A thrill of excitement shot through her the moment her mouth touched his. Quickly she pulled back, her eyes wide as she looked into his face that was still so close.

'And now,' he said softly, 'I think it's up to me to apologise in kind for being the cause of adding to the worry and panic you were already suffering before I spoke to the journalists.'

'There's . . .' no need, she had been going to add, but the rest of it was lost as he claimed her lips with his and fireworks went off in her head that never had she known a man's mouth to be so at once inviting, tempting and, for her sins, so irresistible.

His kiss deepened, both arms holding her securely, tightening when some inner instinct, common sense gone, had her trying to be free. 'Relax,' he instructed quietly, taking his mouth from hers only briefly. 'Nothing is going to happen you don't want to happen.'

His lips on her once more, the warm masculine smell of him, sharp, clean, in her nostrils, had her hands gripping tightly on to his shoulders as she strove desperately to control the wild urges his kisses aroused.

'No!' she protested hoarsely when his lips left hers to transfer to her throat, to kiss across her collarbone and to the hidden swell beneath her dress. Her flesh tingled just before he obeyed and transferred his mouth back to her own, his hands caressing in delicious stroking sensation on her bare arms, moving to her spine, pressing her to him.

For mind-blowing moments his lips left hers to lightly kiss her flushed cheeks, to trail kisses to her ears. And then his hands were in her hair, taking all appearance of sophistication from her as her shining honey-gold hair cascaded over her shoulders.

His look was satisfied as he pulled back to see his handiwork. 'Beauty is an understatement,' he breathed, and the next time his mouth hovered near hers, Perry's lips parted of their own volition to receive his kiss.

'Nash,' she cried his name, when his kiss finally ended,

her arms now about him, all inhibitions disappearing as he wakened ardour in her, 'hold me close!'

Needing no second invitation, with one arm holding her securely close to his heart, the other busy at the zip of her dress, he pressed forward until she felt the solidness of the settee against her.

How she came to be lying down, her dress loose about the top of her, she was too far gone to know or care. Nash's kisses had awakened dormant fires she had been ignorant of, his caresses making her moan from pure pleasure. She was his wife, came the words to quell any last-minute feeling that she shouldn't be like this with him, as he lay down with her his hands caressing her naked shoulders, his mouth moving enrapturingly nearer her breasts.

She wanted to tell him this was her first time as she felt him pick her up in his arms—instinct would direct him to her bedroom door she knew. But she couldn't tell him, and as at the door of her bedroom he paused, his hold secure as he bent to kiss her, the only words to leave her were a submissive:

'I'm glad we're married, Nash.'

The bedroom door was never opened. She sensed a coldness coming to him the moment the words left her— that second before he set her to her feet.

'What's wrong?' she asked, her desire for him giving her no lead to why that warmth should suddenly have left him.

His breathing was as harsh as his expression as he stepped away from her. 'As you say,' he said, his jaw rigid as he moved only to right her dress on her shoulders and hiding from view her half-naked contours, 'you are my wife. When you remember you also have a fiancé, I think like me you'll agree we shouldn't do anything that will make that divorce the harder to come by.'

Everywhere felt cold when he had gone. Even though

burning inside with shame and mortification, Perry sat huddled over her gas fire ten minutes later still wondering what had come over her.

That Nash's blood could have been nowhere as over-heated as hers, that her reminder that they were married had instantly alerted him to how close they were to consummating that marriage, made her want to howl her eyes out from the humiliation she felt.

What had happened to her inner chemistry she had no idea. But she faced squarely that she had been part way to being seduced before Nash had so much as kissed her! That it had been Nash who had been the one to remind her of Trevor, her promise to him, made her cringe with self-contempt.

That Nash was an expert in the ways of getting under a woman's guard was no excuse for the way she had behaved. He had taken notice of her one protest, and would not, she felt sure, have pressed her had she made another protest. But she hadn't. Oh hell! she groaned. He had gone on his way thinking she was as easy as all his other women, and there wasn't a thing she could say in her defence. He hadn't forced her.

Perry buried her face in her hands, wondering how she would ever be able to face him again. Nothing had been decided about the divorce. Nash hadn't stayed above a minute after he had set her down outside her bedroom door. But by the very fact that he had called their love-making to an abrupt halt at the thought of being ensnared into a proper marriage must mean that he agreed to a divorce. He had said, hadn't he, that the divorce would be made harder to come by if they . . .? Oh, God!

Perry's shame and self-reproach had her hurrying to bed and burying her head beneath the clothes as if by doing so she hoped to hide from the misery of her feelings—but sleep was a long time in coming.

By the time morning came, lashed as she had been

through her waking hours, her torment at last found some relief as the thought seeded and began to grow that it hadn't been all so one-sided, had it? Not that Nash would have lain awake for hours mentally whipping himself for his part in it. Not him. He had probably fallen asleep the moment his head touched his pillow. Fallen asleep and slept the sleep of the guiltless.

But it was more than half his fault—the thoughts that had been with her on waking carried on as she sat across from Madge, busy with her needle. She hadn't invited Nash up to her flat, he had invited himself. She hadn't invited him to put his arm around her either. Of course she should have stopped him right there, only in her naïvety she hadn't seen anything sexual, idiot that she was, in having his arm around her; she had seen it more as a comforting gesture. When you knew full well his relationships with women were hardly likely to be platonic, an inner voice sneered at her gullibility. She was saved from further berating herself by Madge enquiring whose turn it was to make the coffee.

'Mine, I think,' and on an idea born of that moment, 'Can you hang on for a few minutes while I pop out and make a phone call?'

That Madge didn't make any wisecrack about her recent habit of slipping out, endorsed for Perry, as she headed for the phone box, what a good sort she was. All she had said was, 'I'll make the coffee. It'll be ready for you when you get back.'

Inside the kiosk Perry emptied sufficient coins from her purse to cover the amount of telephone time it might take her in getting Nash's guardians to put her through to him. She didn't want to be fobbed off by any excuse his telephonist could dream up, the idea of getting what she had to say to him over the phone was much, much preferable to having to say it to him face to face. Already she was churned up inside and doubting after last night's episode if she would ever have the courage to look him in the face again.

'Devereux Corporation,' said that well-remembered voice, and suddenly Perry knew there was only one way she was going to get past it.

'Put me through to Mr Devereux,' she said with all the firmness she could muster. And not waiting for her request to be blocked, she added, 'It's—Mrs Devereux speaking.' Then she found the many coins she had ready in anticipation of a long-drawn-out haggling were not to be needed, as a respectful warm entered the telephonist's voice.

'Certainly. Just one moment, Mrs Devereux.'

Still expecting it would be his secretary Karen Taylor that she would hear next, Perry was nowhere ready to hear that she had been put straight through to Nash.

'My dear,' he said, startling her that his deep voice wasn't anywhere near as cool as she had been expecting.

That was until it came to her that anyone could ring and say they were Mrs Devereux and that that gentlemanly instinct he had mentioned as having was at work, causing him not to call her by name until he was sure of the identity of his caller. The knowledge alone, that despite what he must think of her he was still ready to protect her, thawed some of the ice that had been building up against him.

'It's me, Nash—Perry,' she said, and then heard the coolness in him she had been expecting.

'I intended ringing you tonight.'

Did that mean that he had nothing very pleasant to say to her? His tone indicated as much, and the thaw in her froze over.

'Well, I'm saving you the bother,' she answered snappily. And not waiting to hear why he had been going to ring her—it wouldn't be to apologise for nearly seducing her, she was sure of that—'We didn't get to fully discuss . . .' she hesitated, fairly sure his telephonist wouldn't dare to listen in, but caution coming to her from knowledge of the listening-in tendencies of the telephonist Mr Ratcliffe employed, 'er—the matter we—er—should have done last night.'

'Neither we did,' Nash agreed, which was no help at all, she thought crossly. 'We got sidetracked, didn't we?'

Trust him to have to refer to something she was desperately trying to forget! Her colour pink, her feeling of wanting to put the phone down there and then faded as pride came to help her out. Pride, and a feeling that if he could refer to it when he was more than half to blame, then she was brave enough to refer to it too.

'So we did,' she managed as though she barely remembered it, knowing she was fooling no one but herself, 'and if I remember correctly, you intimated when you left . . .' The pink in her cheeks became a vivid scarlet as she recalled how he had covered up her semi-clad body before saying those words of intimation. She made herself carry on. 'You intimated you were agreeable to—to my—er—request.'

Silence at the other end had her gripping hard on the instrument in her hand. If Nash said no, then she would just *have* to see him again, have to beard him in his office. She had to have it settled, otherwise there was no hope of a future for her with Trevor. The way she had been with Nash last night flashed searingly through her mind, and she was awash with guilt when he finally deigned to reply, his words short as though his time was valuable.

'My intended purpose for phoning you tonight was to tell you I've made you an appointment with a firm of solicitors for eleven tomorrow morning,' he abruptly told her.

'Sol . . .' she began, and as it came home that what he was saying was that the divorce was on, her voice faded, a smile beginning as, not waiting for her to say more, he told her the name of the firm and where she could find them.

'They know the outline of the case. You can rely entirely on their discretion. Once Mr Leighton has seen you he'll contact his out-of-town office and through them my solicitors, who will deal with your settlement.'

'Settlement! I don't want . . .' Perry found her time allowance in speaking with him was at an end as the phone went down in her ear.

Oh, he had to complicate the issue, didn't he, she thought irately, nowhere near to smiling as she came away from the telephone booth. He could keep his settlement—she didn't want his money. He knew that, of course. By his action he was treating her the way he treated his other women. He had soon banished from his head any notion he had had that she was different, she thought, and saw then that this was his way of saying that last night she had proved that much to him.

It further annoyed her, as she went in search of Mr Ratcliffe to ask him for the morning off, that when she should have been able to give at least a small sigh of relief that everything looked as though it would turn out the way she wanted it, she could take no pleasure from it because Nash had muddied it up with the settlement issue.

In view of the many hours she had worked late when pressure of work had demanded it, Mr Ratcliffe paused only to consider the work load they presently had on before he consented to her having the morning off.

'I wouldn't ask, only it is important,' she told him, and was saved feeling awkward that she couldn't tell him more by at that moment being called to take a telephone call from Trevor.

'Ah, you're at work, so you must be better.' His greeting causing her to realise her fake tummy upset must have had him thinking she had been too ill to be at work yesterday.

'Yes,' she agreed, and was glad to leave it at that as he went on to say that having been with his mother over the weekend he was reprieved from his usual Tuesday night duty, suggesting they saw each other that evening— though in case her tummy still wasn't up to it, they would go for a quiet drink somewhere and have a dinner celebration some other time.

Perry's spirits picked up during the afternoon. She as good as had the divorce in her pocket, she thought, and she had seeing Trevor tonight to look forward to. And though there was that in her that said she ought to tell him about Nash tonight, there was a stronger urge that said since she had kept quiet this long, another day wouldn't matter. By tomorrow she might even be able to give him some idea of the date she would be free to marry him.

Trevor was in high spirits when he called for her. And as the evening wore on, visited by guilt for more than her paper marriage, Perry was perhaps showing him more affection than thus far she had allowed—even to the extent that when breaking from a heated embrace when before caution would have had her thinking maybe it was time she went in—alone, she found herself saying:

'Fancy coming in for a coffee, darling?'

Trevor's, 'Sounds promising,' had her biting her lip at the wisdom of her invitation. But it was quickly chased away by the vivid memory of the way she had clung to Nash last night, guilt her tormentor.

'I'll just put the kettle on,' she said as Trevor plonked himself down on the settee. That same settee where . . .

'I don't think you're interested in coffee any more than I am, are you?' he queried, a light in his eyes that should have warmed her, but instead had her knowing that in view of the amorous interlude they had exchanged in his car it might have been better to have invited him in another night.

'Perhaps not,' she agreed, her sights set on the easy chair as she walked back into the room.

'I can't hold you in my arms over there,' he hinted, and

guilt at her wantonness last night was with her again as she smiled and went to sit beside him.

But when Trevor took her in his arms and began to carry on from where they had left off in his car, Perry was shattered to find there was no response in her.

I enjoyed him kissing me a few minutes ago, she thought in bewilderment as she wrapped her arms around him as though just touching him would trigger off the reaction he so clearly expected.

She felt his mouth on hers, felt a roughness in his embrace she had never felt before, felt the tightness of his arms around her increase as desire for her grew in him. But nothing was happening for her! It was as though, she thought, horrified, Nash was still in this room. She felt him there, his unseen presence stultifying any natural feeling she had for Trevor.

'Come on, Perry,' Trevor urged, her lack of response getting through to him as he pulled away to stare at her. 'You were eager enough not so long ago. Why else did you ask me up?'

'I—It doesn't seem right,' she replied, and wasn't surprised when he gave a scoffing laugh.

'For God's sake, you're twenty-four, not fourteen,' he said, trying to pull her back to him. 'We're engaged, for heaven's sake—or as good as.'

It was no good. She knew he could badger at her all night and she just couldn't give in to him. Not here, not in this room. Last night was too close, too well remembered. She stood up nearer than she had ever been to telling him of her marriage secret.

'Trevor——' she began, and turned to face him. Only all at once it wasn't Trevor she saw sitting there. Nash's face, mocking, the devil in his eyes, swam before her, blotting out Trevor's petulant look. 'I . . .' she tried, and finding it hopeless, turned from him to add, 'I'm sorry—I can't.'

To say he had been put out was putting it mildly, she

thought, after he had slammed out and she lay in bed.
Damn you, Nash Devereux, she fumed as she punished
her pillow—it's all your fault!

She was surprised when she awoke to find she had slept
so well. Then recalling the restlessness of her sleep the
night before she thought it wasn't so very surprising.
Though she grew confused when analysing that it ought
to have been thoughts of Trevor whom she loved going off
in a huff, that kept her sleepless rather than the way it had
been, her previous night's sleep ruined by thoughts of Nash
Devereux.

Nash entering her thinking had her getting up and going
to her wardrobe. With any luck today would see the beginning of the end of him. But she wanted to look smart.
Grudgingly she admitted she owed him that much—to
look smart the way one would expect an expense-no-object
Mrs Nash Devereux should look.

She selected a two-piece wool suit of a deep shade of
mustard. She would have to come home and change before
going to work, she mused as she leisurely bathed and,
afterwards, put her hair up. Madge had already guessed
that she was going through something of a crisis in her life;
to turn up at work dressed to kill would give her further
food for thought.

The time when she should be on her way upon her, she
snatched up her portmanteau handbag, shook her head
that it didn't go with her elegant outfit, and realised she
was going to be late if she didn't get a move on. But it
didn't take long to transfer bare essentials, purse, powder
compact, comb and keys, into her more fashionable brown
leather bag.

At the door a last-minute thought hit her and had her
scurrying to her bedroom to remove the top half of her
jewel box. She had better take proof of her marriage, she
thought, her fingers closing on the copy marriage certificate prior to stuffing in inside her bag and looking forward

to the day she could tear it up. Nash's dealing with Mr
Leighton had most likely been done over the telephone or
through his own solicitor. Mr Leighton would surely want
to see the certificate.

Running late of the time she had set herself, for all she
had thought she had ample time earlier, she was further
delayed by Mrs Foster coming from her door out into the
hall.

'Oh, you're all right, then, Perry,' she greeted her. 'I
was getting a little worried about you when I didn't hear
you go out at your usual time.'

'I'm fine,' Perry smiled. 'I'm not going to work until
later I have an appointment. Anything I can get you on
my way back?'

'I'm all right for day. But you could get me some bread
tomorrow if it's no trouble.' Then, remembering Perry
had said she had an appointment, 'But I mustn't keep
you. I expect you're in a rush, the way I always used to
be.'

Poor Mrs Foster, Perry thought, as she made it to the
pavement and began hurrying along. The poor dear,
besides being overweight, had arthritis, which made it
impossible for her to hurry anywhere any more.

Hoping to find a cruising taxi, Mrs Foster went from
her mind as she consulted her watch and saw if she was
going to make her eleven o'clock appointment on foot she
would be better getting on with it rather than keep looking
back for a non-existent taxi.

The solicitor's office was less than five minutes away
when her frequently consulted watch told her she had
about six minutes to make it, provided she didn't meet
any hazard in the shape of an old friend she hadn't seen in
donkey's ages, or get stopped for breaking the pedestrian
speed limit. She smiled at the idea that flitted through her
head of a policeman coming up and asking her number.

Then the notion disappearing, her smile remained as

Nash Devereux entered her head and the satisfaction that was shortly to be hers in the blissful parting that was to come.

She turned, her mind full of it, to cross the road, and met the hazard that was to prevent her from keeping her appointment in the shape of a taxi she had given up seeing—and didn't—as it was furiously braked.

CHAPTER SEVEN

THE pain in her head as her eyelids fluttered open and she regained consciousness made Perry aware all was not well before the cotton wool in her brain cleared sufficiently to make her realise the bed she was in was not her own. She was in hospital.

She coughed and stifled a groan as a pain in the region of her ribs told her something was amiss in that area too. Bread, she thought, trying to recall how she had got to be in hospital. All she could remember was that Mrs Foster wanted a loaf of bread. What had happened after talking with her in the hall, she had no idea.

Needing someone to tell her how she got to be where she was, she turned her head, wincing as a spear of pain came sharper than the bearable dull throb, and closed her eyes briefly before observing, on opening them again, that there wasn't a patient in the next bed simply because there was no next bed. Gritting her teeth against further spasms of pain, she turned her head in the other direction, to see there was no bed there either. She had a room to herself.

Perhaps I'm dreaming, she thought, cotton wool wanting to take over her brain again. But if the aches in her body were anything to go by it was a pretty rotten dream. Sleep wanted to claim her, but she fought it as panic began to take a foothold. She wasn't dreaming, she knew she wasn't, and what was more, she couldn't afford a private room. What were they thinking of putting her in here?

A sound like the crash of dustbin lids in her pain-ridden head had her wincing afresh as a door she couldn't see without turning and inflicting more pain opened somewhere behind her head.

'Good, you're back with us,' said a gentle female voice which made itself known in the shape of a mousy-haired, white-capped nurse bending over her. 'I know it hurts like crazy,' the nurse went on, efficiently popping a thermometer under Perry's tongue and taking her wrist in a cool hold while she took her pulse, 'but I'll get you something for it in a minute.'

Unable to voice any of the questions she was bursting with, with the thermometer in her mouth, Perry was forced to lie docilely while the nurse checked her general appearance before removing the temperature gauge from beneath her tongue and began writing down details on her chart.

'Nurse.' Perry found her voice weak, and not at all as strong as it should have sounded. 'What happened?'

The nurse didn't seem to think it unusual that she couldn't remember, and explained, 'It would appear you stepped off the pavement and came off second best in an argument with a taxi.' And while Perry wondered where she had been, what must she have been thinking about to have been so careless, Nurse Johns, as she later learned she was, quite without knowing it promptly stifled any further questions she might have, by saying, 'Now don't bother your head with anything else, Mrs Devereux, I'll be back in no time with something for your sore head.'

Mrs Devereux! Fear, alarm, panic added to her condition, causing Perry to feel she had just been poleaxed.

'Nurse!' she called urgently.

But Nurse Johns had already departed, and by the time she returned, and an injection was administered with speed and efficiency, Perry's brain was so filled with a complexity of cotton wool padded thoughts that nothing very coherent came from her.

The next time she awoke it was dark, but a dim light showing in the room told her she had not been left unattended. Then as before the door behind her opened, and this time a different nurse appeared.

'How's the head now?' enquired a rosy-complexioned staff nurse.

'Much better,' Perry answered with truth.

'Good. In that case I think we can allow you one visitor,' the nurse said, beaming archly as if to say she knew who her patient would prefer to see above any other visitor.

'What time is it?' Perry heard herself ask, and wondered how much damage had been done to her head that she should be asking that question instead of enquiring who her visitor was. Though perhaps it wasn't so daft, she mused, as the nurse told her it was half past nine. Visiting hour must have come and gone—so she must be privileged to have a visitor at this time of night. Though maybe in private wards they didn't have any strict visiting times.

'Your husband is just having a word with Sister,' the nurse continued brightly, quite happily unaware that Perry was just recalling that the other nurse had called her Mrs Devereux, and with that recollection, alarm made itself felt again.

'N-Nash is here?' she croaked.

'Mr Devereux has been in to see you on and off since you were brought in,' was the smiling reply, 'Now just sit tight,' said the nurse, causing Perry to wonder where she thought she would be going, unable to move without her aching body making her aware of parts of her she never knew she owned before.

Feeling physically beaten, she found her brain came actively alive. If Nash was here, though how on earth they had traced him as her husband, or her as his wife, since the press hadn't been able to do it, then she had every confidence that he would clear up every question that rattled around in her head.

Why she should have such confidence in him she couldn't have said, as she sat tight and waited, though lay would have been more appropriate. But as the minutes ticked by before her listening ears picked up a firm tread halting outside her door, she had recalled the last time she had seen Nash.

And by the time that door was opened, she didn't know how she was ever going to speak to him, her embarrassment choking her, let alone ask him one single solitary question.

But she had reckoned without Nash being able to deal with any situation. Unable to meet his eyes, with nowhere to look lying prone as she was, Perry opted to close her eyes. She heard the small scrape of a chair as he lifted it to the side of her bed, then found her hand taken in the secure hold of his cool large grip.

'You know, Perry,' she heard his even tones, not cool, not sarcastic, teasing maybe, 'if you didn't want to go ahead with the divorce you only had to say. There was no need to half kill yourself to avoid making your appointment with Mr Leighton.'

Her eyes flew open at his teasing, though she was grateful for the shaded light as she met his scrutiny full on. 'Oh, Nash,' she said weakly, then, clarity of thought coming through where before all thoughts had been fuddled and only half finished, 'That's where I was going, wasn't it, to see Mr Leighton?'

He smiled, his hand still holding hers. 'They said you could remember nothing of the accident, though it did seem vitally important to you that Mrs Foster had a loaf of bread.'

Perry smiled too as she wondered if she had been delirious. Then her smile disappeared, a wrinkle of worry on her brow. 'Mrs Foster will be worried when I don't go home tonight. Oh, Nash,' agitation took her, 'I must get word to her!'

'Relax,' he ordered. And if he was observant enough to note the colour that flooded her cheeks at the choice of that word she had last heard from him when he had begun to make love to her, he didn't refer to it. But he made her feel instantly better by telling her he had already been to see Mrs Foster and acquaint her with what had happened.

'Though I'll admit,' he teased lightly, 'she was slightly puzzled when I presented her with the loaf of bread I took with me.'

How easily he can make me smile, Perry thought with wonder. Of course, he made her angry too, she made herself think, her lips straightening, and then as her head cleared, anxiety there again, this time that she might be a permanent invalid.

'What did happen, Nash? What's wrong with me? The nurse said I'd collided with a taxi, but . . .'

'You'll be fine after a few days' rest,' he soon put her mind at ease on that score. 'You were concussed for a few hours, so they want to keep you under observation. But apart from a sore head, a few bruised ribs and the general feeling you've been run over by a juggernaut, you have no need to worry about broken bones or anything of that nature.'

That was so good to know. She was smiling at him again before she could hold it back. But there were other questions she wanted the answer to, and they came tumbling hurriedly from her.

'They're calling me Mrs Devereux,' she said, serious now, anxiety showing once more. 'The nurse, the one who was in here before you came in, referred to you as my husband.'

In her agitation she pulled her hand from his, an involuntary movement that took her finger distractedly to her mouth. In a moment Nash had recaptured her hand, was holding it securely while his other hand soothed the back of it in a calming, stroking movement.

'Oh, where did they get that information from?' she cried, her eyes fixed on him. 'You didn't tell them, did you?'

Her confusion was apparent since unless he was ap-

proached there had been no way he could have known
she was in hospital; he shook his head. 'The copy of our
marriage certificate was in your handbag. It was the only
means of identification you had with you. Since my name
is on the certificate too it was natural they should contact
me. My name is fairly well known,' he added, telling her
something she already knew in a dry-humoured attempt
to draw another smile from her.

But this time she couldn't smile. She groaned instead as
she recalled delaying herself those few minutes by going
back for that certificate. Oh, if only she hadn't!

'I thought Mr Leighton might want to see it,' she
agonised. 'I . . .' she stopped as another thought grass-
hoppered in. 'They've put me in a private room,' she said
worriedly. 'Nash, I just can't afford such a luxury.'

The hand holding hers held firmly as now Perry gripped
on to him. 'Naturally I shall settle the account,' he assured
her quietly.

'No!' Her answer was prompt. 'I couldn't let you.'

'I'm afraid you'll have to,' he said, a hint of steel there
before he checked it and went on more kindly, 'Anyway,
apart from it being me who gave the instructions, and the
account therefore going down to me, a fine Ebenezer you'd
make me look if it came out that I'd let my wife pay her
own hospital fees!'

She knew it didn't matter a damn to him what anyone
thought of him. But before she could say a word to argue
the point, a thought came that was far more terrible than
who should pay when she vacated this room.

'Nash,' she said urgently, the enormity of that thought
almost choking her. 'If everyone here knows who I am,
then . . .' she gulped as she tried to get it out, 'then there
isn't the smallest chance the newspapers won't get hold of
it, is there?'

She knew the answer from the way he looked as though
he wasn't going to answer.

'Is there?' she pressed, her fingers clenching hard on

to his as she waited.

His answer was to bring her hand up to his mouth, and her urgency was momentarily abated as, amazed, she watched and felt his kiss on the back of her hand.

'I'm afraid not,' he said quietly, as gently their hands touched down on the bed cover.

Perry knew then from those three words quietly dropped into the air that it was already too late to try and stop the wheels of the press turning. She tried a deep calming breath that hurt her ribs and was no help at all.

'My accident was reported in tonight's paper, wasn't it?' she asked tonelessly, and saw the answer in his face.

'Yes.'

'As Perry Grainger I'm not very newsworthy, am I?' Her voice was husky, and she was past flinching when after a moment's hesitation he put her out of her misery— by adding to it.

'The headline read, "The whereabouts of the mysterious Mrs Nash Devereux revealed".'

Tired, defeated, she had to ask a weary, 'Do you have the paper with you?'

'No, I don't.' She heard the sharpness entering his voice as he asked, 'Why punish yourself? I've told you all there is to know.'

'I should like to see it.' Even in tiredness and defeat her stubborn streak wouldn't desert her. 'Would you come and see me tomorrow and bring the paper with you?' she asked.

Nash looked as though he was going to refuse. But whether it was because he had intended not to come and see her again, or whether because he knew it was the paper she had to see more importantly than him, she didn't know.

'If that's what you want,' he said, standing up and re-turning his chair from where he had got it, his movements telling her he was about to leave.

'Nash.' He came to the bed, stood looking down at her.

'I . . . I don't want to see—anybody else.' She felt uncomfortable that no word came from him as he stared down at her. She knew he was thinking her a coward for not wanting to see Trevor until she had sorted out what she could possibly say to him.

'I've already given instructions to that effect.' He spoke at last, bringing her gaze quickly away from the bunch of daffodils he must have placed at the foot of her bed when he came in, but which she had only just noticed.

'You have?'

Nash allowed himself a small smile. It charmed her when she didn't want to be charmed. Or perhaps it was the effect of seeing the unpretentious daffodils he had brought her when she would have thought his sophisticated taste would far more likely run to orchids.

'I thought you would want it that way,' he said, showing how easily he could read into her mind.

It confused her that he could get on her wavelength and read her thoughts before she had even thought them. 'Thank you for the daffodils,' she said, to cover her confusion. 'They're beautiful—a touch of spring.'

'Like their recipient,' said Nash, and while her confusion mounted, he leaned over the bed and placed warm gentle lips to her forehead. 'You're like a touch of spring yourself.'

Perry didn't have very long after he had gone in which to wonder at such words coming from the cynic about women she knew him to be. For as if she had been standing outside the door waiting for him to leave, the rosy-cheeked staff nurse was in her room again and she was once more on the receiving end of an injection, this one ensuring she had a full night's sleep.

Her daffodils, now placed in water, were the first thing she saw when she opened her eyes to a sun-filled room. She smiled from pure pleasure at seeing their bright yellow heads.

Her smile didn't linger. Remembrance of where the flowers had come from, all their donor had last night had told her, crowded in, and her head that should have been resting chased this way and that with a problem she could no longer delay in dealing with.

Yet still there was hope in her that maybe the papers hadn't given too much detail about her. Hope grew as she considered the possibility of the report referring to her only as Mrs Devereux. The name Mrs Devereux would mean not a thing to Trevor. Hope spiralled upward. They couldn't have a photograph of her, she thought, and that being so, with just the title 'Mrs Devereux' and no accompanying picture, Trevor might not even bother to read the report.

She was able to smile again when the efficient Nurse Johns bustled in. 'Ah, sitting up and taking notice, I see,' she greeted her cheerfully. 'That's a good sign. We'll have you out of bed for a bath as soon as Doctor Boardman has seen you. Meantime we'll freshen you up with a lick and a promise.'

Her feeling that she might yet be able to confess personally to Trevor what was now becoming her dark secret, before he heard it from anyone else, stayed with her for most the time the nurse attended to her. In any case, with Nurse Johns brimming over with cheerfulness, she found it impossible not to respond.

That was until, her bed made, the nurse remarked that her friends were up bright and early.

'Friends?' Perry exclaimed, mystified, with a suspicion of something akin to fear trying to take hold.

'One or two people have phoned to enquire how you are,' Nurse Johns informed her.

'Who rang—d-do you know?' Fear was concreting. If she said Trevor's name Perry knew she wouldn't rest another minute until the hospital discharged her.

'Your husband for one. Mr Devereux wanted to know

what sort of a night you'd had, and what time the doctor would be seeing you.'

Perry smiled because it was expected of her, but she was less interested that Nash was showing an unexpected concern for her, the reason for which she couldn't fathom unless he thought he had a duty to enquire since he had forbidden anyone else to visit her; what she was more interested to learn, feeling quite sick inside, was the name of her other enquirer.

'That was kind of him,' was all she could find to say about her husband, and adding as casually as she could, 'You said someone else rang.'

'The taxi driver who made you briefly airborne,' said Nurse Johns, smoothing out a non-existent crease in the bedcover. And while relief started to flood through her patient, she added something that sent that relief bolting. 'And a Madge—her merry face frowned as she tried to recall Madge's surname. 'Sorry,' she said, 'it's gone. But a lady called Madge rang to ask how you were.' She went to the vase of daffodils to arrange one that wasn't to her liking and missed seeing that Perry's pale face had gone a shade whiter. 'She said,' the nurse added, standing back to admire her handiwork, 'to tell you Ratty, I think she said, will just die if he thinks he's going to lose you.'

Nurse Johns turned, smiling, her eyes observing Perry's white face, and her smile dipped as she mistook the reason for her patient's lack of colour.

'Now don't you worry,' she said, severely for her. 'Ratty, whoever he is, isn't going to lose you. Neither are we. Why, in a few days you'll be out of here, apart from a few aches and pains as fit as a Stradivarius.'

About to tell her Madge hadn't meant Ratty would die if he thought her injuries were worse than they were, that she hadn't because of the message thought she might precede him, Perry found the explanation too much for her. So she smiled weakly instead, which seemed to please her nurse before she bustled out and on to her next patient.

Oh lord! Perry thought, the moment the door had closed. If Madge knew, if Madge had connected that she was Mrs Devereux, then her name, her full name, must be in the paper. It must mean too that Madge had previously read Nash's statement that he was hoping for a reconciliation with his wife. Madge must have put two and two together, ignoring that she knew of her love for Trevor, and must have decided of the two men she knew who she would choose and therefore, since Perry was reconciled with Nash, Mr Ratcliffe was about to lose an employee.

For the next hour or so Perry agonised over the fact that if her name was in the paper, then it was too late for her to get to Trevor first. So it wasn't surprising when Doctor Boardman came to see her, a tall thin man who looked at her over the top of his half-moon spectacles, that her temperature was soaring and she was confined to bed for the rest of the day.

It was useless telling herself she was doing herself no good by getting churned up. She just couldn't help tearing herself apart when she thought of how Trevor would think she had been two-timing him.

Maybe it was because her brain had to have some relief from the constant thoughts that nagged it that about three o'clock that afternoon, her thoughts swung off in another direction. Maybe her name hadn't been in the paper at all, she thought, hope rising again. Perhaps, when she hadn't gone into work yesterday afternoon, Madge, worried about her, had called at her flat, seen Mrs Foster and from her learned that she was Mrs Devereux!

She clung to her latest theory, not liking it very much, but finding it far more preferable to the only other theory. And at last, for the first time that day, rest essential, brain weary, she nodded off to sleep.

It was still light when she awakened, so she couldn't have been asleep for long, she thought. Then, sensing she was not alone, she turned her tousled head on her pillow and felt shock as she stared straight into the grey eyes of the man sitting beside the bed.

'H-Hello,' she greeted Nash, cobwebs of sleep vanishing rapidly as he didn't appear very pleased to be there, his unsmiling face a fair indication that the kind way he had been with her last night hadn't lasted. He didn't look today in any way as though he thought her a breath of spring.

'Why aren't you eating?' he demanded. 'Isn't hospital food good enough for you?'

Taken aback by his attack, she felt weak tears speed to her eyes before anger with him had them pushed away. If he had come here only to bark at her he could jolly well go away again!

'That's no way to talk to an invalid,' she said, nettled, and saw she had amused him by showing that by no chance had all the stuffing been taken out of her. She saw his mouth quirk, and having felt nowhere near smiling naturally all day, she felt the corners of her own mouth begin to twitch.

'I would have brought you grapes,' he said, his scrutiny of her thorough, 'only I don't like them.'

Perry couldn't resist it. A picture of Nash sitting there calmly hogging all her grapes came into her mind, and she giggled.

'That's better,' he observed. 'I thought we were going to have tears when I first spoke to you.'

'It's your charm that does it,' she said sweetly, and thought she must still be lightheaded that the laugh that came from him was the nicest thing she had heard all day.

'What do you fancy for supper?' he enquired, and she knew then he was aware that tears weren't so very far away and was playing a lighthearted game with her to keep her spirits up.

'Smoked salmon to start,' she joined in, 'followed by—er—cauliflower cheese and mashed potatoes, and black-currant cheesecake to finish up with.'

The game ended suddenly. 'So what went wrong today?' His question fell quietly, but she didn't miss that he looked determined to have an answer.

'I don't know what you mean,' she replied, feeling not unlike a pupil in front of the headmaster for some misdemeanour.

'Throughout the night you were checked,' he enlightened her, his sternness not letting up. 'At eight o'clock this morning you were doing fine. You should have been up and about today, but Dr Boardman's examination of you gave him cause to ring me to . . .'

'Dr Boardman rang you?'

'I'm your husband, remember,' she was sharply reminded.

'As if I could forget!' she returned smartly—and knew from the way his mouth firmed that he had only just controlled some angry retort. She saw then his eyes taking in what her mirror had that morning shown, that she looked washed out, and heard his voice calm, gentle almost, when next he spoke.

'What happened after eight this morning, Perry? Aren't you going to tell me?' he coaxed.

'You—you should have put a block on telephone messages as well as visitors,' she blurted out, her stubbornness melted by the unexpected gentle coaxing where it would never have done had he remained looking ready to bite her head off. 'As well as the taxi driver ringing to enquire how I was, my friend Madge from work rang.'

She didn't have to add any more. Nash's brain took it from there. 'So you've been stewed up all day with thinking if your friend Madge knows you're Mrs Devereux, then your—boy-friend must know it too?'

Dumbly she nodded. 'He'll hate me for not telling him, I know he will,' she fretted.

'He takes an evening paper, does he?'

'Sometimes,' she answered absently. 'But even if he

didn't have one last night, I'm sure he'll ring my place of work today. Madge doesn't like him,' she inserted, her pale face growing anxious as the thought came. 'I'm not at all sure her loyalty to me won't be put to the test when she's up against the urge to tell him—to tell him . . .'

'You love another,' he put it.

'Hardly,' she snapped, embarrassed that he might be thinking what she was thinking, that her love for Trevor hadn't been much in evidence that night Nash had started to make love to her.

She heard his exaggerated sigh, saw his face was easy, as lightly he quipped, 'I must be slipping.' But she wouldn't smile, so he went on, perfectly serious now, 'Would you like me to see him? Explain how . . .'

'No,' her answer was rapid and certain.

'Good,' he said, 'I might well have ended up telling him to leave my wife alone.' And while she stared at him in amazement, he thought briefly before explaining, 'I rather think friend Madge is a better judge of character than you are.'

'You know nothing about Trevor Coleman, or his character,' Perry found enough strength to hotly defend him.

'I know he has you scared of him,' Nash bit back, making her eyes nearly pop as he let her know he didn't think much of men who frightened women, having no idea that when she was eighteen he had scared the life out of her. And anyway, she wasn't afraid of Trevor! Of telling him her secret maybe, but . . . 'I know he lacks a certain decisiveness when it comes to making up his mind about proposing to my wife,' he went on. And if she wanted to be flattened with embarrassment, which she didn't, he made no bones in telling her, 'And from your point of view he can't be any great shakes as a lover, otherwise you wouldn't have been so ready to go to bed with me as you were.'

'You pig!' she snapped, her face crimson, tears of mortification very close to the surface.

For a moment there was complete silence in the room, Perry's swallowing gulp as she fought for control breaking it. Then, as he had done last night, Nash took her hand in his. She wanted to tell him to go, to leave her alone, but was afraid to speak again until she was sure she wasn't going to cry.

'I am, aren't I?' His quietly agreeing to her short statement she thought him a pig had her tears drying. But she wanted to get off the subject of him as an expert lover, and fast.

'You didn't bring last night's paper as you promised,' she accused, changing the subject rapidly.

'Who said I didn't?'

He released her hand to dip inside his jacket pocket to show he had brought the cutting with him. A cutting he had obviously not been going to show her unless she asked to see it.

She took it from him, not certain now that she did want to see it. Slowly she unfolded it, saw the headline he had last night told her about, 'The whereabouts of the mysterious Mrs Nash Devereux revealed'. Perry read on, unconscious that her hand was again held by a much larger one. Despair was with her when she reached the end, the cutting fluttering from her hand to the bed cover, her worst suspicions confirmed.

'Oh, Nash,' she said mournfully, tears she could no longer control streaming down her face. 'If—if they'd taken it all from the marriage certificate they couldn't have been more word-perfect, could they?'

One moment Nash was sitting on his chair by the bed, and the next he was balanced on the bed beside her, an arm about her as he pulled her head to rest on his shoulder.

She held on to him simply because, lacerated by her thoughts as she had been all day, it was the last straw to see in print that Perry Bethia Grainger, a seamstress, had married Nash Devereux just over six years ago. She needed the comfort afforded by that strong firm shoulder as she just sat there and wept.

With a gentleness she found unbelievable Nash cradled her to him, only releasing her when at last her tears dried. When, his eyes still kind, he took out his large handkerchief, mopped her up, and as if she were a six-year-old, ordered her to, 'Blow.'

Her water-washed eyes looked apologetically back at him as he studied her face, the mopping up operation completed. 'I'm sorry,' she said softly.

'The apology is mine,' he told her, making no move to take his arm from the back of her. 'I didn't want to see you in tears,' he admitted slowly, 'but perhaps they'll have some healing effect.'

Bemused that she actually did feel very much less tense than she had, as much as by the fact that Nash saying he hadn't wanted to see her in tears indicated a weak spot for a woman's tears she would never have attributed to him, she accepted that he was right. Even with his arm around her she was much less knotted up inside than she had been.

Belatedly, it came to her that for a girl who had a fiancé, she shouldn't be cuddling up to Nash this way, and had to wonder then what it was about him that seemed to make his arms a natural haven. Charisma? she wondered. Whatever it was, Nash had it by the ton. And right at this moment she was in danger of revising her opinion that she didn't like him very much, for he had shown her a side of him she hadn't thought existed.

'I'll be all right now,' she said, straightening away from him, suddenly very much aware, ridiculously, that in her hospital nightshirt, no make-up and with her hair a mess, she must look a sight.

'That sounds very much as though I've just been issued my marching orders.'

'Well, you must have loads of things you want to do,'

she answered, feeling she might have sounded a little un-gracious after the way he had patiently borne seeing her flooding the place.

For answer he dropped a light kiss on her forehead the way he had last night. 'Be good, Perry Devereux,' he said, 'I'll see you tomorrow.'

Perry Devereux indeed! she thought after he had gone; but not for much longer. Though her light head had a lot to answer for in that, at that moment, it didn't make her cross that he had called her by that name. It had, she thought tiredly, rather a pleasant ring to it.

Her smile came naturally again before the day was finished. Still lacking in appetite, she found her appetite tempted when her supper was wheeled in, in the shape of smoked salmon, cauliflower cheese with mashed potatoes, and blackcurrant cheesecake.

'It was delivered from outside,' said the girl who had brought it in.

'I know,' Perry gurgled even before she found the note that was attached to the most exquisite arrangement of primroses, '*Bon appétit*. N.,' it said. 'My husband sent it in.'

CHAPTER EIGHT

FEELING tired enough to believe she wouldn't have any trouble in getting to sleep, Perry refused the offer of a sleeping tablet and consequently wakened frequently during the night.

She had to admit that since Nash's visit she felt less panicky, less strung up. But that didn't stop her from worrying about Trevor, of how he must be feeling.

After another fraught wakeful session, dawn about to break, she came to a decision, her conscience at last telling her what she must do. She closed her eyes once more, common sense advising that her plan could not be put into action until the doctor had been on his morning round.

Nurse Johns bustling in with her usual enthusiasm had Perry opening her eyes to discover she felt rested, and though still very tender in places, very much better.

'Ah, that's what I like to see,' the nurse chirruped. 'Nice clear eyes and looking ready for breakfast.'

'I'm starving,' Perry lied, looking away from her favourite nurse as she started on her plan to appear perfectly fit when she told the doctor she wanted to sign herself out of his care, his hospital.

'Excellent!'

Her temperature taken, Perry tried to sound casual as she asked, 'Ninety-eight point four?'

'Nearly normal anyway,' Nurse Johns replied. 'You'll be able to have that bath today, I'm sure.'

Perry wanted her bath before she saw the doctor, not afterwards. But left with a bowl of water and the necessary equipment she was able to give herself a thorough wash when Nurse Johns was called away.

Disturbed to find that so little physical effort, the

twinges from her bruises with each movement, had exhausted her, she lay back, knowing she would need the few hours' rest before the doctor came, to rebuild her strength.

When Nurse Johns returned, busying herself with tidying up, Perry forced a brightness to reply to anything she had to say. But she waited until she looked ready to depart, then as casually as before, asked:

'By the way, any idea where my clothes are?'

'Fed up with nightclothes already?' the nurse smiled. 'They're not far away. Though if you're thinking of sitting out in your day things after the doctor has been I wouldn't advise it. A couple of days in bed, not to mention a bump like the one you suffered, can be more weakening than you imagine.'

'I feel fine,' Perry protested, knowing the truth of what was said.

'That's the ticket,' said Nurse Johns as she disappeared through the door.

By the time Dr Boardman, with Sister and Nurse Johns in attendance, came to see her, she was feeling well again. She had even convinced herself it was ridiculous to lie there occupying a hospital bed someone else might want to use. That her determination to leave the hospital that morning had anything to do with the way she decided she felt, she didn't give a thought to as she waited patiently as the doctor ran his rule over her before proclaiming that she would be as right as rain in a couple of days.

Anticipating a sticky time, she had a stubborn look on her face as the moment came to tell him she wasn't waiting those couple of days.

'I feel well now,' she told him, sending him a smile because she had been so well looked after and would hate any of them to take it personally. 'In actual fact I—er——' she stumbled on embarrassed but determined, 'I've decided to go home this morning.'

Dr Boardman began to shake his head, and seeing a

'you must learn to walk before you can run' dialogue
coming, she invented crazily on the spur of the moment
and hoped nobody remembered the date of her marriage
reported in the newspaper.

'It's my—our wedding anniversary today.' And this
time hoping the doctor had read, and remembered reading
of the reconciliation Nash hoped for, she further perjured
herself when she saw that though still looking doubtful he
was no longer shaking his head. 'It's very important to me
that—that I'm with my husband tonight,' and going red
at what that statement implied, she rushed on, 'that—that
I dine with him in our home like the night we did when
we got married, I mean.' She came to a halt, unused to
lying, knowing she had come to the end of her inventive
powers.

For long moments Dr Boardman said nothing, but just
stood and surveyed her from over the top of his glasses
while she hoped and prayed he had a soft heart and that
she wouldn't have to leave the hospital without his bless-
ing.

'It seems to me,' he said at last as she waited with
baited breath, 'that if I say no to your request, the start
you've made to recovery is going to take a setback.'
Wordlessly she stared at him, not daring even to smile.
'Are you going to promise me to take plenty of rest if I let
you go, Mrs Devereux?'

'Oh yes, yes,' Perry said eagerly, her smile coming
readily.

'In that case Sister here had better telephone Mr
Devereux to tell him he can . . .'

'No!' She saw mild astonishment at her sharp 'No' in all
three faces looking down at her and hastened to explain,
finding she hadn't used up her powers of invention after
all, 'I want it to be a surprise. Besides,' she thought to
add, 'my husband is out of town today and won't be back
until early this evening.'

Victorious, but in quite a lather at all the whoppers she

had told when everyone trooped out, she was smitten too by conscience about Nash. She faced that he had been good to her while she had been in here. He needn't have bothered about coming to see her, for one thing, let alone see she had a private room. He had said he would visit her today, about the same time as yesterday, she judged. Would he be angry when he arrived and found her gone? Or, which was more likely, would he think thank goodness for that, and then sit back waiting for the divorce petition to reach him?

She frowned to realise that all thoughts of the divorce had gone from her mind while she had been in hospital, then her brow cleared. She had had too much else to worry about, hadn't she?

Nurse Johns came in with her clothes and helped her to dress, her manner saying that while the professional side of her disapproved of Perry's leaving before she was properly ready, the heart of the woman that beat beneath her uniform thought it the most romantic thing she had heard in a long day.

'You sit there,' she said when, keeping the fact that she felt whacked to herself, Perry was ready. 'I'll just go and see about your taxi.'

Fortunately Perry didn't have far to walk to the taxi, but having refused the use of a wheelchair she found she was glad to have Nurse Johns supporting hold on her arm. Then she was in the taxi, listening to her nurse instructing the taxi driver firmly not to just deposit her and drive off, but to see her safely indoors.

Warmly thanking Nurse Johns for all her care, Perry waved to her despite her creaking muscles as she raised her arm. And only when the hospital was out of sight was she able to breathe a sigh of relief, and lean forward to instruct the driver where she wanted to go.

'They said at the hospital that it was Belgrave Square I was supposed to take you to,' he grumbled lightly.

'Must have got me mixed up with someone else,' she

said, careful not to meet his eyes in the driving mirror. Belgrave Square must be where Nash lived.

He was kind, her taxi driver. Though whether it was because she was looking as all in as she felt, or that he was just following Nurse Johns' instructions, she didn't know. But he helped her to the front door and even inserted the key she had· got out ready when paying him inside his taxi.

At the sound of the front door being opened, Mrs Foster limped into the hall, and after one look at Perry she came as fast as she could towards her, and her ample arms were round her, giving her a hug.

'Oh, love, I've been so worried about you!' she exclaimed. And standing back, she cried, 'You don't look well enough to be out of hospital. They must need the beds very badly to send you home looking so poorly!'

'I'm fine, Mrs Foster,' Perry told her with more determination to be fine than with truth, 'honestly.'

'Well, you're not tackling those stairs until you've had a sit down and a cup of tea,' Mrs Foster insisted, 'that's for certain.'

Inevitably during the fifteen minutes she sat in her landlady's living room, the subject of Nash had to come up.

'I couldn't believe it when he told me he was your husband,' said Mrs Foster, to which Perry sent a silent 'thanks a million, Nash', until it came to her that with almost everyone else seeming to know, probably it was just as well. She wouldn't want Mrs Foster hurt that she was the last to know. 'I mean, you've never said anything in all the time you've lived here.'

Feeling guilty, and not liking the feeling, Perry placed her empty cup and saucer down on the table in front of her. 'I was trying to forget it,' she said gently, and saw an understanding in her landlady's face that came from her experience of life over the years.

'These things happen,' she shrugged, 'separation, divorce. But he's such a nice man.'

Perry smiled, because there just wasn't any answer she was up to making to that. She got to her feet, thanking Mrs Foster for the tea, declaring she felt ready for anything, and asked if she could use the phone. She might as well get it over with now as go up to her flat to brood on it and have to come down and make the call anyway.

'Of course you can, you know that.'

Perry dialled Trevor's place of work, all thought of what she was going to say to him going from her mind as she waited for the call to be put through to him.

'Perry?' His voice didn't sound very welcoming.

'Trevor, I . . .'

'Where are you?' he cut her off.

'Home, at my . . .'

'I'll come round.'

Staring at the phone as it went dead, she knew apprehension. Trevor had sounded in a filthy mood, he hadn't even asked her how she was!

Mrs Foster came out of her living room as she replaced the receiver. 'All right, dear?' she enquired.

'Trevor's coming over,' Perry told her quietly.

She saw Mrs Foster's face was sombre as she guessed, 'He didn't know about Mr Devereux either, did he?' Perry shook her head and saw understanding back in Mrs Foster's face again as she said, 'You go on up. I'll let him in.'

She didn't have to wait long in order to let Trevor in. Before Perry had got herself half way composed, she heard him at the door. Heard him coming up the stairs, and he was then bursting in through the unlocked door before she could get to answer it.

Pale, shaking when she saw the ugliness in his face, she knew before she started that he had no interest in any explanation she had to make.

'You deceiving little tramp!' he snapped, slamming the door after him, taking no heed that she looked rocky on her feet. 'A fine fool you've made me look!'

'Trevor, I—I meant to tell you, to explain . . .' was as far as she got.

'Everybody's laughing at me behind my back!' he shouted at her, coming over and wrenching at her arm, making her wince as he caught one of her tender spots, and unheeding he ranted on, 'Mr X, that's what they're calling me at the office!'

'How could they know?' she tried, none of his colleagues known to her.

'How could they know!' he repeated as though he thought she was stupid. 'Because I was misled enough to think I was engaged to you—told them at work I was engaged to a Perry Grainger. Told them your middle name because it's so unusual. I even told them the sort of work you do!'

'Oh,' said Perry, her head starting to ache as his downturned mouth took on a sneer.

'Oh! Is all you can say, is it? No apology at the laughing stock you've made me!'

'I'm sorry, Trevor. Honestly, I'm so very sorry.'

'Not as sorry as you will be, my girl,' he threatened. And at that moment all resemblance to the Trevor she knew, the Trevor she knew and loved, disappeared as he yanked her off her feet and half threw her on to the settee.

Wide-eyed, disbelieving that this furious-looking man, that ugly expression on his face, just couldn't be the man who had asked her to marry him, she fought dizziness as she pleaded:

'Listen to me, please listen!'

'What for?' he snarled, his lips going moist as his eyes roved her. 'I've heard all from you I want to hear. "No, Trevor. I can't, Trevor," ' he mimicked nastily. 'Wanted to keep your virtue until we were married, did you?' he sneered. 'And all the time your virtue had been had by another man—more than one, I shouldn't wonder!'

Still unable to credit it—this couldn't be her Trevor?—Perry tried to get up from the settee, only to find she was pushed down again as he joined her, his hands grabbing roughly at her jacket.

'Well, let me tell you, Perry Grainger *Devereux*,' he spat the last word, 'I'm not asking you to give in this time. This time I'm taking what's mine. And you can forget anything I ever said about wanting to marry you. Why should I? I don't need a preacher to give me permission to take what you've been withholding from me!'

His meaning was only too clear, and she saw there was no trying to reason with the madman he had become. Her body shaking, she tried to move out of his range. Panicking, wildly she tried to push past him. But her strength weakened, puny, was useless against the maniac that raged inside him.

She felt her jacket pulled uncaringly from her as Trevor caught her and threw her back on to the settee, heard her blouse tear as she tried to fight him off, heard herself pleading, 'Trevor, don't—I can explain . . .'

'Explain it to your husband,' he rasped, his hands brutally tearing at her skirt. 'Reconciliation!' he scoffed. 'He won't want to know you when I've finished with you.'

Perry opened her mouth to plead again, but breath went from her as the weight of his body landed heavily on top of her. And then all thought of pleading with him went as breath returned and instinct had her using it all with what strength she had to start screaming.

'Shut up, you bitch,' Trevor grunted, transferring one hand from her clothing to smother her mouth.

His head came nearer as his hand left her mouth, and then several things happened at once. Before his mouth could touch hers the sound of a door being crashed in reverberated through the room, while simultaneously she

started again to scream. And then her scream was shocked
into silence as she felt the weight hauled off her, and
watched stunned as Nash's fist shot out and sent Trevor
flying through the air.

What Nash was doing there, where he had come from,
was more than she could cope with, then as her head spun
dizzily she saw undismayed that several pieces of her furniture would be in need of repair where Trevor had crash
landed.

Ignoring him, Nash turned to her. She saw a frightening
livid fury in his face as he took in her shocked, ripped and
torn state, but she was past wondering if she looked as
ashen as she felt.

'You look ghastly,' he gritted, not bothering to dress it
up. 'Did he . . .'

'No, no, I'm—all right,' she managed, fighting hard
against the dizziness that was turning her world grey.

She saw his contemptuous gaze flick to where Trevor
was trying to regain his feet. She felt as ghastly as he said
she looked when she saw the expression on Nash's face,
and through mists gathering in her brain had a distinct
impression that murder was about to be committed.

She tried to call Nash's name, to stop him, but no sound
came save Trevor's blubbering attempt to save his skin as
he too witnessed from Nash's expression that he would be
lucky to get out of there with his life.

'She had it coming,' he croaked.

Nash went forward, 'You *bastard*!' he spat as he
advanced.

'She had it coming,' Trevor repeated, fear in his voice
as he backed away and tried to excuse himself.

'You . . .' Nash called him another name that should
have shocked Perry, but didn't, as he followed his prey
across the room.

'She's been playing me along for months.' Perry saw
Trevor's eyes feverishly searching for a way of escape just
as mists of grey swirled up around her, 'making out she

was a virgin when she's known one man at least! His rising voice reached her as Nash grabbed him by his lapels. 'Don't . . .!' Trevor squealed. And it was at that point that her struggle to stay conscious ended.

All was quiet when she came round. Her eye lids fluttered open to discover she was still on the settee but now had a blanket covering her. A movement at the side of her had her recognising Mrs Foster. Where Nash or Trevor were she didn't know, but fear at what had been about to take place before her faint had her asking agitatedly:

'What happened?'

'You fainted,' Mrs Foster told her gently, and as she tried to sit up, 'Don't move. Mr Devereux has gone for the doctor. He said you were to lie still if you came round before he got back.'

'Doctor!' Perry exclaimed, and felt too weak suddenly to argue. Though her feelings for Trevor were all muddled up at that moment she just had to find out what had happened to him.

'Trevor,' she whispered fearfully, half dreading she would be told Nash had killed him. 'What happened to him?'

Mrs Foster's face was a mixture of grimness and satisfaction. Satisfaction faded the grimness as she revealed, 'I'd just reached your landing on my way up to see what the dickens was going on when all at once I had to make myself very small,' she smiled at Perry trying to encourage a smile at the thought of her overweight size instantly reducing itself. But Perry was past summoning a smile, so she went on, 'Well, all at once Trevor came hurtling out of your door propelled by Mr Devereux, who didn't even wait to see if he'd broken his neck as he threw him down the stairs and then disappeared into your sitting room again.'

'He hadn't broken his neck, had he?' Perry queried, hating any form of violence and dreading the worst.

'No such luck,' said Mrs Foster uncharitably, causing

her to see that like Madge she had never liked Trevor, but unlike Madge, had kept it to herself. 'I wanted to find out what was going on, since you must be in some trouble. So I stayed there only long enough to see that young man crawl out on all fours—in a hurry, from the way his car took off—then I came in, to see your husband trying to bring you round from a faint.'

Still feeling faint, Perry wondered how long she had been out, since her landlady had mentioned something about Nash going for a doctor.

'I could see for myself that you'd been attacked,' Mrs Foster continued—a brief reference to Perry's torn clothing. 'Mr Devereux went and got a blanket from your bedroom, explaining a bit of what he saw when he came in. I told him I wished I'd given him a helping hand in throwing Trevor Coleman down the stairs, for all he didn't need any assistance from me.'

'I'm sorry for all the upset, Mrs Foster,' Perry apologised, 'I never imagined Trevor . . .'

'Good gracious, you've got nothing to apologise for,' she answered stoutly. 'I just thank God Mr Devereux called when he did. You started to scream just as I'd opened the front door to him. He was up the stairs before I'd got the door shut.'

The sound of someone entering the house had Mrs Foster moving her stiff joints to leave the chair Nash had placed for her by the settee. Then Nash and another man about the same age came into the room, and Nash came straight to look down at Perry.

'I won't ask how you're feeling,' he said abruptly, 'I can see.' His tone alone without the disgruntled look of him told her there was no time in his life for the sordid scene he had been made a party to—endorsing, as his glance flicked away, that he couldn't bear to look at her, that the sooner the doctor had checked her over and he could be gone the better as far as he was concerned.

Then he was introducing his doctor friend Daniel Hepwood to both her and Mrs Foster, surprising Perry out of her idea that he had found the whole scene nauseating in the extreme, something he didn't want to be associated with, by saying:

'This is Perry, my wife, Daniel,' claiming her as his wife to his friend, and introducing her as such. 'I've explained about the accident Perry was in and the attack on her a short while ago. Mrs Foster and I will wait downstairs while you check her over.'

As soon as they were gone Perry tried to protest that she was fine, that she didn't need to be checked over. But when Daniel Hepwood drew back the blanket and saw the marks of fresh bruising starting to show through her torn clothing, his face revealing nothing of his thoughts, he gave her a winning smile.

'Would you have old Nash having my guts for garters?' he enquired teasingly, and she had to give in.

She had had enough today, she thought as she answered questions, had a light shone in her eyes, her pulse taken. She didn't think she could take Nash charging up here and laying down the law about what was best for her—it was much easier to give in.

'You'll mend,' Daniel pronounced, pulling the blanket up over her. And, with his ear cocked towards the open door, 'Ah, methinks I hear the rattle of the tea-cups. Fancy one?'

She did, though she felt guilty when he went down in hoping he would be the one to bring her up a cup, and so taking up more of his valuable time. But Mrs Foster had already been up once, bless her, and she didn't want her disabling herself with a second journey up those steep stairs. Nash, she thought, even if he had stayed to hear what Daniel Hepwood had to say, wouldn't stay longer.

While she waited, she put her will power to use. She felt better now, she told herself. She would leave the settee in a minute, go and change. She would rinse her face, brush her hair, that would make her feel better, and—and tomorrow she would get down to doing some serious thinking. Today it was beyond her.

She heard firm footsteps on the stairs, and had a smile on her face ready to thank Daniel not only for the tea he was bringing, but also for dropping everything and rushing round at a moment's notice.

Her smile disappeared as Nash, balancing a cup and saucer on a tray and looking as though he was very unused to the task as he endeavoured not to spill any, entered her sitting room.

'I thought you'd gone,' she said without thinking, relief flooding in that although his eyebrows went up, there was a suggestion of a quirk to the corner of his mouth that could mean he wasn't about to lay into her.

'Now why should I do that?' he asked, taking the cup and saucer from the tray and handing it to her. 'What sort of a husband would I be if I left my wife alone on—our wedding anniversary?'

The tea slopped over into the saucer, a drop falling on to the blanket as Nash's hand came out to steady it. Seeing she was over her start, he took the seat previously occupied by Mrs Foster and then Daniel Hepwood.

'Er—you—er—phoned the hospital?' she asked, not needing his reply.

'I thought I'd enquire how you were doing,' he answered.

Would she never lose this feeling of being guilty over everything she said or did just lately? Perry wondered, knowing she had metaphorically been caught with her hand in the till and couldn't lie her way out of this one.

'It worried me—Trevor,' she explained, owning up. 'I th-thought—realised last night that by not telling him . . . By letting him find out about . . .'

'Leave it,' Nash instructed, seeing she was struggling. 'It's not important.'

She turned grateful green eyes to him. She owed him the explanation after he had so kindly arranged that private room for her, but if he thought it wasn't important, then at that moment it was good enough for her.

'Daniel gave me a couple of sedatives for you,' he announced, his voice easy. 'Do you want to save some of your tea to help them down or shall I get you a glass of water?'

She had taken them before she realised Nash was being quite masterful. He hadn't given her the chance to decide whether she wanted to take them or not, but had merely emptied them into her hand and leaned forward to ensure that she did so.

But when he said, 'All right if I act as lady's maid?' visions of him calmly stripping her and dressing her in fresh untorn clothing had her thinking he was going very much too far.

'Thank you all the same,' she said primly, 'but I can manage to change quite well by myself.'

'Foiled again,' said Nash, and Perry had the most unladylike impulse to take a swipe at him when she saw him grin wickedly. 'To be more precise,' he said, 'I was asking your permission to pack a few things for you.'

'Pack!' She was glad this time her cup was empty as it rattled in her hands before he took it from her. 'Pack what? Where do you imagine I'm going?'

It had taken a lot of effort for her to leave hospital and get this far. If he had any bright ideas in his head of packing her a case, and by the look of him he had every intention of doing that with or without her permission, and taking her where, she couldn't begin to think, then he could jolly well think again!

'How,' he said, undisturbed by the determined look of her, 'how does the idea of spending a few weeks in the country appeal to you?' And not letting that idea do more than lightly touch the surface, 'I know of a delightful house in darkest Sussex where you'll be able to rest and regain your strength before you start to take up life again.'

She wasn't going to go. She wasn't. Even if it did sound like heaven. 'Whose house is it? she asked suspiciously.

'Mine.' He was serious as he went on, 'I've already phoned Mrs Vale, my housekeeper. She'll have a room ready for you by the time we arrive.'

'Perhaps when *you* arrive you'll extend my apologies to Mrs Vale,' Perry said stubbornly. 'I'm going nowhere with you.'

She looked away then, not liking that his face took on an expression that looked more determined than her own. She wouldn't look at him even when, after a lengthy pause, he enquired quietly:

'Frightened, Perry?'

'Frightened?' she exclaimed, and was suddenly terribly unsure of herself. In a way Nash did frighten her. Oh, not his mannerisms, his bad temper with her on occasions. Certainly not that time he had kissed and caressed her— God, she'd made a fool of herself then—but something about him, what she didn't know, had some inexplicable instinct warning that she might end up suffering more pain than she was at the moment—if she went with him.

'You've just received a shock of the worst kind.' His voice was quite still, a hint of gentleness there. 'I hadn't intended to refer to it, but if what happened to you— might have happened to you,' he corrected, 'has affected your trust in men, then be assured I would never attack you in such a way.'

She was gasping as he came to an end of what he was so seriously telling her. 'I know you wouldn't!' she said, shocked that he could think she doubted it.

'You trust me?' he asked, and looked pleased when she nodded.

She did trust him, she thought, her brow wrinkling. Bewildered that even having trusted Trevor, never having given thought that he could do what he had, not knowing

Nash nearly so well, for some unknown reason she just knew he wouldn't so vilely attempt to abuse her.

'I thought you were going to kill him,' she said, following her own train of thought, and finding Nash had no trouble in following her.

'It was on the cards,' he said, his tone hardening. 'Had you not chosen that precise moment to moan and pass out . . .'

'Mrs Foster said you threw him down the stairs,' she remembered. 'Why—why were you so angry, Nash?'

There was a brief pause before he replied, his eyes taking in her exhausted face, the sedatives at work, the lassitude showing. 'Wouldn't any decent man have done the same?' he asked in reply. Then he rose from his chair, suddenly the man of action that he was.

Tiredness went from her briefly as she wondered where he was going when he went from the room. In seconds he was back, her jeans and sweater in his hands, telling her he had made a second trip to her bedroom.

'You can change in here while I get your things together in the other room,' he told her, clearly expecting no argument.

'I'm not going,' she found the will to protest, and had to watch as Nash hid the exasperation he must be feeling with her when bluntly he told her:

'You're not fit enough to be on your own and you know it. And before you say you're not on your own, that Mrs Foster can look after you, you'll accept with the honesty that's in you—give or take a few acceptable lies in the circumstances—that it takes that good lady all her time to potter about her own place without further crippling herself half a dozen times a day by climbing upstairs to see if you're all right.'

He was right, of course. And she wouldn't dream of letting Mrs Foster come up at all. She wouldn't have let her come up earlier had she been in any position to stop her. But still her stubbornness persisted.

'I'm not coming with you, Nash, and that's final,' she said.

'Very well,' he agreed, and she knew a brief moment of victory. That was until he added smoothly, 'If you'd like to get changed, I'll run you back to the hospital.'

Open-mouthed, she stared at him, stubborn green eyes looking into hard unrelenting grey eyes. 'I'm not . . .' she tried.

'Take your choice,' said Nash to a girl who, for all their kindness to her in hospital, would rather be anywhere than go back, 'hospital or Sussex?'

Perry drew a tired breath of defeat, but felt too weary suddenly to fight him any more. 'Swine,' she said dispiritedly.

'You say the sweetest things,' said Nash.

CHAPTER NINE

Snuggled beneath the blanket Nash had tucked around her before they started out on the drive to his country home—Greenfields he had told her it was called—Perry battled against the desire to sleep.

'Fighter to the last, aren't you?' Nash commented suddenly, making her aware that while most of his attention was on his driving, he still had time for the occasional glance her way and had just caught her forcing her eyelids apart. 'Why not give in?' he suggested mildly. 'The journey will be less wearying for you if you close your eyes.'

The surviving spirit in her wanted to tell him she wasn't tired. But he had already found her out in one or two blatant lies, and she knew he wasn't going to believe this one anyway.

'I promise to keep it to myself if you snore,' he remarked, causing her lips to twitch when she wanted to feel indignant.

'I thought you lived in Belgrave Square,' she said out of blue, something that had occurred to her when he had first mentioned his country house. Then, afraid he might think she had been checking up on him, 'That's where the taxi driver wanted to take me from the hospital, anyway.'

Nash didn't comment on what he thought of her countermanding the taxi driver's previous instructions, but told her after a moment, 'It's convenient to have a flat in London. But having been brought up in the country I like to have the wide open spaces around me whenever I get the chance.'

Surprised and a little pleased that the hard man she had known had opened up to reveal a little of himself, Perry found herself asking softly:

'Does it upset you, Nash, that Lydia inherited your old home?' and immediately she had, she wished she hadn't. Perhaps he was still bitter about that time six years ago.

'That bang on the head doesn't appear to have affected your memory,' he observed, smoothly overtaking the car in front. Then after a moment's silence when she was still wishing she had bitten her tongue and slightly pink that he was going to ignore her question, he said, 'No, it doesn't upset me. It was my father's wish that she should have it—that he couldn't see her for what she was was my bad fortune.'

Perry saw more in his answer than he said. He meant he saw it as his bad fortune that he had had to go against all his deep-seated convictions about ever marrying, in order to get what was so rightfully his.

Unconsciously she sighed. Nash could have done something ages ago about his bad fortune in having to take a wife. She wished he had. None of what had taken place would have occurred had he divorced her long, long ago. As it was, life as she had known it would no longer be the same. She had lost Trevor, and, suddenly feeling weepy, she wasn't sure that losing him bothered her all that much—which was confusing, because he had meant so much to her. Perhaps the heartache would start tomorrow, she thought, sighing again. At the moment she felt too numb from all that had happened to feel pain anywhere but where she had been physically hurt.

A small yawn escaped. Her eyes closed. She'd open them in a minute, she thought . . .

The next thing she knew was that strong arms held her, and were carrying her, plus blanket, away from the car. It was still daylight and for a second she didn't know where she was. Then above her she saw Nash's face, dark hair whipped by a gust of wind in an engaging cowlick across his high, intelligent forehead.

Grey eyes spotted that she had awakened as their owner

progressed over a gravelled drive, a manservant preceding him to open doors. 'Hello, Nash,' Perry whispered, still half asleep, and felt an idiot as his eyes showed amusement. That was until he said gravely:

'Hello, yourself.'

A thin wiry lady nearing her sixties greeted them in the hall. Perry guessed she was Mrs Vale as she told Nash everything was as he requested, and asked if she could be of assistance.

Ignoring Perry's movement suggesting she was capable of standing on her own two feet, he held on to her as he thanked Mrs Vale, suggesting, 'Perhaps you'll come up in about fifteen minutes with something to tempt my wife's appetite, Ellie.'

Then as his housekeeper went away to do his bidding, he carried Perry up the stairs, passing the man he called Bert coming from the light airy room Nash took her to.

Without saying a word, he placed her on a velvet-covered chair while he went to unplug the electric blanket he had obviously ordered to be switched on.

Perry watched, thinking she should make some comment. But seeing his thoroughness in action as he went over to her suitcase that Bert must have brought up, she was lost for words as she saw him extract a nightdress which he had thought to pack at the top, knowing it would be wanted first.

Her eyes followed him as he placed her pink satiny nightdress on the, just then, most inviting double bed she had ever seen, and then he came over to pull her to her feet.

'Come on, Sleeping Beauty,' he said matter-of-factly, his fingers already at the welt of her sweater ready to pull it over her head, 'it's bed for you.'

But while she still felt tired enough to welcome bed, she certainly wasn't *that* tired that she was going to stand for him confidently thinking he was going to be the one to undress her, impersonal as he seemed to be.

'I can manage by myself,' she said, pulling her sweater down when already it was level with her bust.

'Oh dear, oh dear,' said Nash, sarcasm about to break, she knew it. It didn't come. With a resigned sigh he lifted her until she was sitting on the bed. 'Get busy with the top half,' he instructed. 'I'll be back in a few minutes.'

For all her tiredness, careless of her aches and pains, Perry had her nightdress over her head and was struggling to pull her jeans from her legs when, in under a minute she was prepared to swear, Nash reappeared.

Studiously ignoring him, her face pink, her arms purposely covering the front of her, she got on with her task. Then she found Nash wasn't looking at her as he came to bend to her shoes, remarking:

'Didn't Nanny ever tell you it's easier if you take your shoes off first?'

'I never had a nanny,' she said sourly.

'Nor your bottom slapped either, by the sound of it,' he commented, delegating her straight to the nursery as her shoes came off and she had to sit while he pulled her jeans from her ankles. 'Anything else to come?' he enquired, and there was a devil in his eyes, she saw, as he read in her eyes that he could go and take a running jump before she'd remove her briefs.

Wisely he didn't wait for her answer, but pulled back the covers and had her tucked up in the luxurious warmth of the bed, when ease came instantly to her aching body.

'Hmm, this is delicious!' she sighed blissfully, forgetting to be sour as the heat salved her wounded flesh. 'Pure heaven,' she purred, saw the look of utmost satisfaction that came to him, and didn't care at all then that he looked to be pleased that he had done the right thing in bringing her to his country home.

Then suddenly he was saying, 'I won't be around to

keep an eye on you. Please me by staying in bed for the rest of the day.'

'Where are you going?' she asked promptly, knowing she had no right, but comfort leaving her that it looked as though he was prepared to dump her in his home and then disappear.

'A man has to earn his crust,' said the man who headed a multi-million-pound empire. 'I have a meeting in London this afternoon.'

'Oh.' Having lost all sense of time, Perry wanted to ask if he intended coming back or was he spending the night at his flat in town. But that feeling of guilt was smiting her again. 'I'm sorry, Nash. You—I must have cut heavily into what must be a very busy day for you.'

He gave her a look that conveyed 'all in a day's work' but didn't stop longer than to tell her briefly that if he wasn't too late getting home, he would look in on her, and while she was still trying to hide the smile that piece of information evoked, he went.

Not understanding why she should feel so gladdened he was returning to Greenfields that night, Perry snuggled down in the bedclothes, no longer feeling like sleep, more—floaty.

She came round from her floaty feeling when Mrs Vale brought her up her lunch. And for all she hadn't thought she was hungry, she suddenly felt ravenous as a delicious smell of home-made soup reached her. She took an immediate liking to Mrs Vale, who insisted she call her Ellie as she adjusted her pillows, thinking that for all Ellie's size being in direct contrast to Mrs Foster, she was just as motherly.

'Feeling sleepy?' she enquired, taking the last of her dishes away and looking approving that she had made quite a good showing of eating most of her meal.

'Not a bit,' said Perry, feeling wide awake.

She realised very shortly, when Ellie came back after

taking her used dishes away and pottered about unpacking
her suitcase before asking her if she would like her to sit
with her for a while, that Nash must have left instructions
that she wasn't to be left alone to brood.

Though she was grateful to him that he couldn't have
said anything to her about what had happened to her
after she had left hospital when Ellie, waving aside her
suggestion that she must be more than enough extra work
without taking up any more of her time, drew up a chair
to sit near the bed and remarked:

'Nash said you shouldn't be out of hospital yet, so you
must share some of his determination that having decided
you wanted to leave you got them to telephone him to
come for you.'

'They were marvellous to me,' she said, grateful to Nash
for keeping the sordid business to himself, 'but . . .'

'But like me you can't abide such places,' Ellie smiled.
'Well, we can look after you just as well, Mrs Devereux,
only you'll have to take things very easy. Though Nash
will see to it you don't overtax yourself.'

That sounded very much as though she was in for some
more of his bossy treatment! Perry made up her mind
there and then to make her recovery the fastest on record.
Nash had said she should stay in his home for a few weeks,
but a few days, she thought, were going to be enough if he
was going to start acting the lord and master.

For the next thirty minutes or so they chatted idly and
comfortably on any subject that presented itself, Perry
telling about her work and hearing that Bert was Ellie's
husband, and earning a warm smile from Nash's housekeeper when after she had called her Mrs Devereux several
times, a name Perry was not at home with at all, she asked
her to call her by her first name the way she did Nash.

By the end of that time Perry had realised from Ellie's
way of speaking of Nash, the affection there in her voice
whenever his name cropped up, and from the way she

referred to him by his first name, that she must have known him before he had bought Greenfields. And since by now they were getting on with each other famously, she was able to put the question:

'How long have you known Nash, Ellie?'

'My name was the first word he spoke as a baby,' Ellie replied proudly, and went on to reveal, her loyalty to Nash never in doubt, that she and Bert had been in service to his parents. 'His mother was such a lively soul,' she remembered. 'Said she couldn't stand being buried alive in the country.' Her eyes saddened. 'Nash's father was never truly happy after she left him.'

Recalling that Nash had as good as said his father had been besotted with Lydia, Perry couldn't stop the, 'But he married Lydia,' that rose to her lips.

'An old man's fancy,' sniffed Ellie, leaving her in no doubt that she didn't care very much for Nash's step-mother before she went on. 'She wanted Bert and me to stay on and work for her, but not likely.' Her last three words spoke volumes. 'As soon as she moved in, we moved out. Nash found us when he bought this place and since we weren't much happier in the job we'd moved to, we couldn't start to work for him soon enough.'

There was an amiable silence in the room for a few seconds; then suddenly Ellie was showing surprise that Perry knew of Lydia's existence at all, asking was it Nash who had told her about her. And when she confirmed that he had, she saw the momentary look of puzzlement on her face as she said:

'Nash never talks about his father's second wife,' then, her face magically clearing, 'I'm sorry, I haven't got used yet to the fact that you and Nash are married. Naturally he would discuss things with you he wouldn't discuss with anybody else.' Her face was solemn as she added, 'None of us knew Nash had a wife. We only learned it from the papers. Oh, I do so hope everything goes well for you from now on, that the reconciliation he's hoping for happens.'

'We . . .' Perry began. But feeling such a liking for Ellie even on such short acquaintance, she just didn't have the cruelty in her to dash that look of fervent hope she saw in her face by saying, 'We're going to be divorced.' 'We shall have to wait and see,' she said, and didn't feel so much of a coward when she saw Ellie was smiling again the smile that was so much a part of her.

Then Ellie was standing up and saying that with all their talking they could both do with a cup of tea, pausing to ask if she would prefer something else. Perry knew she meant did she have a preference for coffee, but just had to tell her that what she would like above anything was a bath. Whereupon she discovered Ellie wouldn't hear of her having her bath unattended, and ten minutes later was exclaiming in shocked tones when she saw the extent of the bruising on her body.

'They should never have let you go,' she said, frowning—and Perry couldn't tell her that she had collected a few more bruises after she had left hospital. 'I don't know what Nash was thinking of in agreeing to such a thing,' Ellie tut-tutted.

'Don't be cross, Ellie,' said Perry, beginning to wish she had done without her bath after all, and saw the housekeeper's frown disappear at her plea.

Though still pale after her bath she felt so much better she was able to eat most of the meal Ellie brought to her at dinner time. Only this time, careful though Ellie had been before when she adjusted her pillows, Perry noted the extra care she exercised, and knew the bruises she had seen were well to the front of her mind.

Sleep came naturally after that, and she didn't fight it. Nash would be home later, and if Ellie went on to him about her bruises the way she had to her, then she would rather be asleep than have him coming in and demanding to look at them—or worse, if heated argument ensued, have him taking her back to hospital.

A nightmare woke her in which Trevor's face loomed huge, misshapen, contorted. She turned on her bedside light and was out of bed as though trying to escape before her fear left her. She checked her watch. Only ten to three and she was wide awake, knowing she wouldn't sleep again for hours.

She moved towards the window, intending to look out, for all it was dark, as she wondered if Nash was home yet. Probably, she thought, but who knew what hours he kept. Then a sound behind her had her spinning round.

The man she had been thinking of stood there. His robe, appearing to have been hastily dragged on, and by the look, over nothing, had her enormously aware of her own scant covering.

'All right?' Nash enquired, quietly closing the door and coming over to where she stood momentarily paralysed. 'I thought I heard you scream.'

He was talking calmly, easing the agitation her eyes were showing at having him there in her room, naked under his robe, she knew now as she saw the hair coming up from his chest as he drew nearer.

'The light beneath your door made me think you might be awake.' They were standing almost toe to toe when still in that same calming voice, he asked, 'Did something frighten you, Perry?'

'I . . .' she began, the dryness leaving her throat, 'I had a bit of a nightmare. I—didn't know I screamed. Sorry I woke you up.'

'Coleman?' he queried, her apology brushed aside. 'Did he figure in your nightmare?'

She nodded. And not wanting to dwell on it, her voice husky, 'I'm over it now. F-forgotten most of it already.'

She thought then he was going to take hold of her in some touch of comfort to chase the rest of her nightmare away. His hands did come up, but only reached as far as her arms, then they were dropped as he took hold of both her hands in his.

'I noticed the bruises on your arms when I was here before,' he said, letting her know why it was her hands he was holding, letting her know too that there was very little his eyes missed. 'Ellie tells me the bruising on your body is far more extensive.' She braced herself for what was coming. 'Was I wrong to bring you here? Should I have taken you straight back to the hospital?'

'No, Nash,' she said, suddenly able to speak freely to him. 'I'm very fair-skinned, so it's natural I should bruise easily. And . . . and anyway, I don't like hospitals.' And in case he wasn't going to take heed of what she said and intended to take her there anyway, 'Please don't make me go back. The doctor—your friend Daniel, he said I was all right, didn't he?'

'He said you should have rest and care,' he told her, his eyes scanning her face.

'Well, there you are, then. I've rested all day and Ellie is caring for me as though I was a day-old chick.'

That brought a semblance of a smile to his face. 'And you're going to rest again tomorrow?' he enquired.

'In bed, you mean?' she asked, not liking the idea very much.

'In bed,' he confirmed.

Perry didn't know why she was giving in so easily. Nash couldn't *make* her go to hospital, any more than he could make her stay in bed tomorrow if she didn't want to.

'Oh, all right,' she said, not very graciously, she had to admit.

But he wasn't offended. Well, he wouldn't be, would he? she thought, growing mutinous because it wasn't like her to be so acquiescent with him and she wasn't liking herself very much. He had got his own way *again*, so why should he be offended?

'How about bed now?' he suggested.

'I'm not tired.'

'Would you be if I went down and warmed a glass of milk for you?'

'I don't like warmed milk.'

'Nor having your bottom smacked either,' said Nash, making her aware she was pushing it.

But he'd done it again. Her smile came out suddenly and sunnily from her mutinous face. 'I wouldn't mind a cup of tea,' she said in apology. And then, thinking by way of an apology after all he had done for her—half killing Trevor topping all she owed him—it wasn't enough, and her eyes misted over. 'I don't know why I'm being so argumentative. It's not like me—I'm sorry, Nash.'

'It's not like you because you're not you yet,' he said kindly. 'You've been frightened by a nightmare—parts of it still fresh in your mind. That's probably why you don't want to get back into bed.'

'I love your psychology,' she said. And as though to prove him wrong, not seeing until later it was what he intended, she went over to the bed, forgetful for the moment that close up he could see very little of her in the nightdress that tended to cling wherever it touched. 'Oh,' she said, seeing his eyes on her when at the bed she turned to give him a cocky 'So there!' look. Without thinking about it she dived in among the covers, almost crying out loud at the pain that shrieked through her.

Nash didn't look smug, he looked concerned if anything as he saw her wincing expression, but his voice sounded smug as he said, 'That'll larn you!'

'Pig,' she said, and didn't mind when he leaned over to put her covers straight that he placed a gentle kiss on her mouth, then asked as quietly as he had when he came in:

'All right?'

'Fine,' she told him, and saw his lips curve that, feel

half dead though she might, she wasn't going to let anyone know it.

'Sugar?' he asked, and Perry felt quite lighthearted as she quickly recalled that he was going to make her a cup of tea.

'No, thanks,' she smiled, and lay down after he had gone, curled up on her side, her eyes closing as she wondered why she had ever been afraid of him. He was quite nice really, given he did have a sharp side it was better not to tangle with. He had been ready to murder Trevor anyway. But would he really have spanked her rear end as he threatened? The answer came back—yes, yes, he would. But he hadn't, she thought. When it had looked as though things were going to cut up rough she had smiled at him, backed down, and he had been kind to her.

She awakened at dawn to find her bedside light still on and that a cup of cold tea was standing there, and she felt awful that after going downstairs in the dead of night to brew up for her she had been asleep when Nash had come back.

Had he stayed to see if she stirred? she wondered, not sure she liked the idea of him watching her while she was asleep, for all he must have seen her unconscious in the hospital. Or had he merely come in and gone straight out again, leaving the tea in case it was only a light doze she had fallen into?

The next time she woke up she felt as good as new. That was until she uncurled her body and stretched and an 'Oooh!' escaped her.

Yet whoever heard of anyone lying in bed on a Saturday? On a weekday, yes, when one was obliged to get up to go to work, the bed pulled then occasionally, especially on those dark winter mornings. But if that sunlight she could see was anything to go by, it was a beautiful spring day out there.

Perhaps Nash would have business in London today,

she thought hopefully, her promise to him of last night weighing heavily, hope in her heart that she might be able to wander outdoors for a while. Well, he hadn't got where he was by keeping a five-day week, had he?

In a mind to have her bath unattended anyway—the thought of Ellie's distress, for all her caring, was something she didn't want if her bruises hadn't faded any this morning—Perry found her idea thwarted as just as she was about to flip back the covers, Nash walked in.

The business suit of yesterday had gone, she saw at once, and gone too went her hopes of spending any time outside, to see that this morning he was trouser and sweater-clad.

'You're not going to London today?' she enquired, wishing she had waited to give him a polite good morning before rushing in headlong to find out what his movements were. She could see from the hard look on his face as he approached that she had been far too eager with her question.

'Wanting to get back to London already?' he said toughly, misreading her completely. 'I would have thought you'd have had enough of that—animal's company to last you a lifetime.'

Oh, how easily he could make her angry! It was on the tip of her tongue to say Trevor wasn't an animal, just for the sheer perversity he aroused in her.

'It was partly my own fault,' she snapped instead, privately of the same viewpoint, that Trevor's behaviour had gone far past the expected limits of civilised humanity. 'I invited trouble,' she added, seeing Nash wasn't sweetened at all that she was taking this line in defending the man who had felt the sharp edge of his knuckles.

'Oh, sure,' he scorned, acid aggression striking her ears. 'What did you do, lie there and say "I've been a bad girl—here I am—rape me"? Your screams sounded genuine enough from where I heard them.'

'Oh, go to hell!' she flared, wanting to cry at how easily

he could flatten her, her spurt of anger blowing itself out, her voice wobbly as that whole nauseating scene came back. 'I—I was terrified, you—you know I was.' She sniffed and searched for a handkerchief from under her pillow, then felt the mattress go down as Nash's weight had him sitting near her.

His voice had lost its hardness as she wiped the few weak tears away. 'So why do you want to go back to London?' he asked gently.

'I don't,' she answered, 'Well, I do, but . . .' Suddenly she found it impossible to lie to him. 'But it's you I want to go to London.' And, unable to look at him, she heard herself confess, 'I was hoping to get up when your back was turned.'

His laugh made her feel better. 'Wretched female,' was all he said, and she found she quite liked him with his face creased in amusement. That was until he added, 'That small shower that just came down tells me you're not as fit yet as you think you are. Wouldn't you agree?'

'Do you always have to be so right?' she asked, knowing she would die rather than let anyone see her in tears if she was well.

'Always,' he said imperturbably, not a scrap put out that she was ready to be snappy again. 'How about if you rest this morning, and if you feel up to it sitting out in that chair for an hour or two this afternoon?'

Wanting to be sarcastic, Perry looked at the chair he indicated, then found she was too grateful for this small concession to say anything that might have him changing his mind. Then she discovered he wasn't waiting for her answer but had stood up and was about to go. Her eyes caught the tea cup and saucer on the bedside table.

'Er—Nash,' her voice stayed him. 'Er—thanks for the tea.'

'Pleasure,' he said briefly, and went. Neither of them had alluded to the fact that she had been asleep when he had brought it and that it was still there as he had left it, only now cold.

Being generally fussed over by Ellie, Perry had her bath and breakfasted, and alone once more, settled back to read some of the magazines Ellie had brought her, saying Nash had gone out by himself before shutting himself with his work in his study.

He *is* kind, Perry thought, none of the print in front of her being absorbed, as the magazine fell from her hands on to the bed. It must be a real pill to him that she was under his roof at all. Yet he had brought her here simply because he knew she didn't want to go to hospital and Mrs Foster was unable to look after her.

Again she made up her mind to get better quickly. She might, if she could find Nash in the right mood, even get him to take her back to London when he went on Monday. He wouldn't want her under his roof those few weeks he had spoken of, she was convinced of that.

He came in to see her again after lunch, but she thought better then than to tell him what was in her mind about Monday. First let him see what excellent progress she was making, she thought, as he came to the foot of the bed, picked up her dressing gown and handed it to her.

'The moment you've been waiting for,' he announced. 'Put that on and tell me where you want to sit.'

'By the window,' she said promptly, obeying his instructions, knowing his not asking her if she felt up to it could only mean he had found out from Ellie that she had eaten every scrap of her lunch.

She had her dressing gown on by the time he had carried the chair to the window, padded it with a blanket to wrap round her and had turned round.

'Just one thing,' he said as she was about to leave her sitting position on the edge of the bed. Grey eyes pinned her as she waited to hear what was coming. 'Just how much of your lunch was disposed of in the bathroom?'

Her pink colour showed her guilt. Though how he knew, as nice as the meal Ellie cooked had been, her stomach wasn't used to more than one big meal a day and a good half of it had been emptied from her plate and flushed down the loo she didn't know.

'Oh, you!' she sighed, exasperated, half afraid that for all his preparations he was going to change his mind about letting her sit out. 'Do you have to be so clever?'

Her answer was a grin that so transformed the sternness of him, she nearly fell flat on her face. 'It's a gift,' he said, adding, 'Come on,' when she was still unsure if bed was to be her place for the afternoon, 'let's see what sort of a job you make of walking unaided.'

It was an effort, in view of the twinges that had a go at her, to walk with her shoulders back. But she managed it, and was rewarded by his muttered, 'Game to the last!' as he tucked the blanket around her and went to bring up a small table so she should have her magazines near should she want them.

She glanced through the window—and her glance stayed. The wide open spaces Nash had spoken of as needing spread out there before her.

Her, 'Why, it's perfect!' came involuntarily as she stared, held by the view. Green fields, sloping land. Trees, some in clumps others interspersed with a hedgerow patchwork. To the right a sizeable coppice, to the left more tall stately trees, not another house in sight.

Nash came to stand by her shoulder, looking, she thought, in the same direction as herself as he remarked, 'Glad you like it.' But for all his comment had been easy, suddenly she was aware of tension, where before there had been none.

She turned her head quickly, sunlight glinting on the gold of her hair, and saw he wasn't looking at the view but at her. His eyes went from her mouth to her hair, and back again to her mouth. And in that moment, Perry knew Nash was going to kiss her.

Her mouth dried. Her heart began to race, nowhere near certain she didn't want him to kiss her. Every womanly instinct was telling her his kiss wouldn't be that same brief meeting of lips he had saluted her with last night—this would be more in the nature of the kiss that had grown and grown that night in her flat. That night she had wanted more!

'Nash,' she said, her voice all strangled and a stranger to her.

At once his expression altered. The sound of his name on her lips, the look of half fear, half wanting was clear for all to see. He turned away, at random picking up one of the magazines from the table and thrusting it into her hands, his honesty defeating her as he wouldn't pretend that tense moment hadn't happened.

'Read,' he instructed grittily. 'Apart from the fact your emotions must still be haywire from that episode yesterday, it wouldn't do either of us any good to let our biological urges get out of hand.'

That snapped her quickly out of her trance. 'You're so right,' she came back pertly, only just holding back 'as usual', wanting to tell him he'd be so lucky it should get that far that she would ever let her *biological urges* get out of hand again. She tried to think of something brilliantly cutting to add, but by the time she had, Nash had been gone a full five minutes.

The couple of hours sitting out of bed were completely wasted, she considered, when Ellie, no doubt sent by Nash, came to help her back to bed before serving her from the tea tray she had brought in with her.

Perry hadn't enjoyed any of it. All she had done was rail silently against Nash that he could so unbalance the steadiness of her emotions just by looking as if he wanted to kiss her. And when she hadn't been railing against him she had been lashing herself with the thought of how it could be that he disturbed her so, when up until yesterday she had been in love with Trevor. And more punishing self-analysis—did she still love Trevor?

It was a fresh shock to discover that no, she did not. Yesterday she had thought it was because she felt numbed that there had been no feeling in her for the man who had shown an ugly side to him. But she was no longer numbed, and couldn't help wondering, had it been his attack on her that had killed her feelings stone dead? Or was it that she had never loved Trevor so wholeheartedly as she had thought anyway?

CHAPTER TEN

PERRY checked her watch when she wakened in the same
bed she had slept in for the past nine nights, saw it was
nearly seven and decided she would stay put for another
half hour. As it was Sunday she suspected Ellie liked to
have a lie in, and though she felt well enough now to go
down and make a start on the breakfasts, knew Ellie would
frown over such an action.

Both Ellie and her husband Bert had been so kind to
her, she reflected, recalling Bert had taken her into the
nearest shopping centre with him on Friday when he had
gone. He hadn't wanted to, she'd known that, she thought
with a smile, remembering his, 'I can bring you back
anything you're short of,' just as if he had known Nash
hadn't bothered packing her cosmetics.

'Please, Bert,' she pleaded, and saw his glance at Ellie
for guidance.

'If you're sure it's not going to be too much for you,' he
had given in at last. But she hadn't missed the way he
watched over her like a mother hen, going with her and
waiting while she selected a lipstick.

Everybody had been wonderful to her, she mused. Even
Nash, when she had thought she would get very short
shrift from him after that episode a week yesterday. That
episode when he had as good as told her with his '. . . it
wouldn't do either of us any good to let our biological
urges get out of hand' that like that other time he was still
ruled by his head and wasn't about to do anything to
make their divorce the harder to come by. Oddly, though,
with the many conversations she had with him since, the
subject of the divorce had never had an airing.

She hadn't expected to see him again that Saturday,

and had not. But Sunday morning he had strolled into
her room as though nothing out of the way had taken
place, his manner easy as he had asked how she was. So
easy in fact she had forgotten she was going to have her
nose in the air the next time she saw him, and had found
herself replying, her manner just as easy, 'Fine, thanks.'
Though she hadn't forgotten she was determined on going
home the next day. 'So well, in fact,' she'd added, 'I think
I'll go back tomorrow.' She had said the wrong thing; she
knew it as straight away his mood had changed.

'For God's sake,' he had barked, 'you can't still be
hankering after Coleman after what he tried to do to you.'

Stunned that he was thinking she couldn't wait to get
back Trevor, she was speechless for a moment, then she
felt her ire rise and was ready to hold her own.

'Trevor has nothing to do with it.'

'No?'

She knew in that one hard spat out word that he didn't
believe her. 'No,' she snapped, 'he hasn't,' and glared at
him, mentally getting her sleeves rolled up for the right
royal battle that was to come.

Only it didn't come. Unexpectedly Nash's expression
relaxed, and he'd perched himself on her bed, his eyes
laughing even if his mouth wasn't.

'Right, little Miss Fury,' he said calmly. 'Tell why,
after agreeing on Friday to spend a few weeks in the peace
and serenity of the country, you've suddenly decided—
after less than forty-eight hours—you've had enough.'

'I . . .' she began, trying to remember when it was she
had ever *voluntarily* agreed to anything he suggested.
'Well—there's my job, for one thing,' she blurted out. 'I
have to get back to work. Mr Ratcliffe . . .'

'Mr Ratcliffe won't be expecting you to return for two
weeks, if then,' Nash told her with the air of knowing
something she didn't confidently.

'He won't?'

'I put through a call to him on Thursday acquainting him with the details of your accident.' He smiled suddenly, and she didn't know whether to smile with him or hit the smile from his face when, with a great deal of charm, he said, 'I thought you'd like me to do that for you.' And before she could draw breath to ask her next question, he answered it just as though he understood she was wondering how he knew who her employer was, 'Mrs Foster told me where you worked.'

Flabbergasted, not wanting to admit the dry way in which he delivered statements had the strangest knack of making her lips want to twitch, solemnly she stared at him.

'For all you're feeling "fine",' he went on, seeing she hadn't anything to come back with, 'I doubt you'd be able to manage the stairs up to your flat without feeling ready to collapse at the top.' And going on with logic she couldn't fault, damn him, not to say playing on her conscience, 'Mrs Foster disregarded the great pain it caused her to climb the stairs to you once before. Do you honestly believe she wouldn't again brave her disability to investigate your wellbeing if she thought you were too quiet up above her?'

He had won easily, then, though she had brought the subject up against last Thursday—the first day she had been allowed to have dinner downstairs. But before she had got properly started he had smoothly headed her off—so smoothly that even now she wasn't sure if it had been deliberate or not as he had apologised for being late home, going on to tell her how one of the directors, an arthritis sufferer, had been at a meeting that day when he had seized up through sitting too long—that word arthritis getting to her. Since he was unable to drive himself, it had been Nash who had driven him home, thereby delaying his own arrival home.

Expressing her immediate sympathy for the stricken

director, Perry had recalled the days when Mrs Foster's
bones seized up and she had needed help. And as Nash
had gone on to regale her with some amusing incident,
the idea of asking to go with him to London tomorrow
had faded.

I *will* ask him to take me home tomorrow, Perry vowed,
seeing it was now twenty past seven and deciding she'd
had enough of bed, and she collected the clothes she was
going to wear and headed for the bathroom. Some of her
bruises had gone, others were fading. And though in all
truth she wasn't sure she felt up to tackling a full day's
work, she was certainly fit enough to be back in her own
home. *And* able, she felt confident, to impress on Mrs
Foster that she had no need at all to worry about her and
make what must be an agonising journey up the stairs.

Her mind set on tackling Nash without delay, Perry, in
smart fawn corduroy pants and brown jersey shirt, left her
room, pausing only briefly on her way downstairs to
admire the fine oak panelling, the magnificent pictures
placed here and there, more intent on finding Nash. She
found the breakfast room empty, but turned undaunted,
determined to seek him out, only to meet Ellie coming in
having heard her and ready to serve her breakfast.

'I was looking for Nash,' Perry said, after greeting Ellie,
who always had a smile for her.

'He's been in his study since before seven,' Ellie told her
warmly. 'Catching up, he said, when I told him he ought
to leave his office at his office.'

Her plans knocked on the head by the knowledge that
Nash wouldn't be in a very receptive mood if she interrupted him while he was working, Perry wondered if he
ever gave work a rest.

'Does he live in his study every weekend?'

'Bless you, no,' said Ellie promptly—which cheered
Perry to think he did rest sometimes. Though why it should
bother her that his nose wasn't always to the grindstone,

she couldn't fathom. 'It's only because you're here that he's behind.'

'Me!' Perry exclaimed, having not a clue how she could be the culprit. She didn't see Nash during his working day, for one thing. And though she thought of him often during the day—she frowned as she realised the truth of that thought—she was positive that, once enmeshed in his work, he never gave her another thought. 'I never see him until he comes home!' she further exclaimed.

'That's it,' Ellie pounced, not making her any the wiser. Then she added, 'Until he brought you to Greenfields we never saw Nash from Monday to Friday, since he preferred to work late into the night if need be so he could have most weekends free at home.' Smiling broadly now, Ellie went on, 'As you know, he's come home every night this week.'

'So the work he hasn't stayed to finish at night has been piling up,' Perry said slowly, seeing very clearly, more guilt added to her conscience, the inroads she had made into his time.

'I know which he would rather do,' said Ellie, her cheerful good humour telling Perry she thought that in his view the Devereux Corporation could go hang if Nash had to choose between it and the intended reconciliation he wanted with his wife. 'Would you like breakfast now or did you want to go in to see Nash first?' Ellie asked, not seeing she had given Perry more than enough food for thought.

'I'd better have breakfast since Nash is so busy,' she replied, and didn't believe it when Ellie told her Nash wouldn't mind if it was she who disturbed him, that he would be delighted to see her.

After she had eaten she wandered about outside, musing that she had plenty to thank Nash for, that to say she wanted to leave couldn't sound any other than ungrateful. Oh, why did everything have to be so complicated?

As she had not strayed very far from the house her eyes ranged over the acres of tree-strewn land Nash owned. It was so lovely here any other girl would be thrilled at the idea of being able to stay another week—so why wasn't she?

Aimlessly she dawdled over the gravelled drive, ruminating on the question. Then all at once, gasping suddenly, an answer came—an answer that shook her to her very foundations, and had her standing stock still.

Still gasping at the unwanted truth going round in her head, in her heart region, she stared unseeing at the scene that moments before had enchanted. The answer rocked her. She had to leave, leave before it was too late! Go now—or she wouldn't want to go at all!

Shattered, Perry stood unmoving, facing the reason why Nash occupied so many of her thoughts. Why he was able to make her laugh as often as he had this week. Why the chemistry in her had her not only firing up at him angrily from time to time, but why that same chemistry had had her melting in his arms as far back—and just then it seemed aeons away—as the time she had thought she had been in love with Trevor.

She hadn't been in love with Trevor, that positive knowledge came hurtling in. But if she didn't look sharp and get out of here, she stood a very good chance of facing the worst heartache of her life! She, unutterable idiot, was half way to falling head over heels in love with Nash Devereux—the husband who had strength sufficient to kill the headiest physical desire at the merest hint that he might find himself married for real.

Some hours later, knowing she would be called to account if she didn't present herself in the dining room, she thanked her guardian angel that Nash was still working.

'Nash is having his meal on a tray,' Ellis informed her. And beaming brightly, 'But he said he was nearly through. So you'll still have a good part of the day to spend together.'

Managing the best she could to find a smile, Perry tucked into her melon and grapefruit starter. She had swung from a very definite intention of seeking Nash out and getting her departure date settled, to now being afraid to face him in case when she saw him the message she suspected her heart of transmitting to her brain turned out to be terrifyingly true.

She didn't linger in the dining room, the ridiculous notion playing on her nerves as she refused coffee that Nash might take it into his head to leave his study and come to share a cup.

It was these same nerves attacking that had her going out the back way so she shouldn't have to pass his study, afraid as she was of bumping into him if his work was finished.

Her nerves threatening to get out of hand she entered the rear courtyard and saw Bert so engrossed with his head under the bonnet of his A40 he would have no idea had she gone by without speaking. But she liked Bert, and stopped, hoping a few moments spent in idle chat might have a calming influence on her agitation.

'Spot of trouble?' she enquired, wincing for him as his head shot up and came into contact with metal. 'Sorry,' she said quickly, thankful it was more a tap than a bang his head received.

'Not really,' Bert answered, always seeming to have time for her. 'Though I fancy a new air filter wouldn't come amiss.'

Perry found him easy to talk with and listen to. Bert carried on with his servicing as he told her he was meeting a fellow model railway enthusiast in London next Saturday, that they were going to an exhibition, and that he wanted to make certain the car would behave itself on the way.

Feeling much less anxious some ten minutes later, about to go on her way, all at once Perry was back to feeling full of anxiety again. For round the corner of the house, a jacket over his arm, hers if she wasn't mistaken, came Nash.

Manlike, he poked his head beneath the bonnet of the A40, passing comment to Bert, then turning to Perry observed by way of explanation for the jacket in his hands:

'When I couldn't find you downstairs I went to your room. Coming for a walk?' and obviously not expecting any answer but yes, he held her jacket up for her to put her arms in.

No, said her head. 'Yes, all right,' she heard her non-objecting heart answer. And before she could change her mind she found he had taken hold of her arm and was walking her away from the house, telling her they wouldn't go far and she must tell him immediately she began to feel tired.

'I'm not an invalid,' she protested, not knowing who she was most cross with, him or herself.

'You're not in a very good mood either, are you?'

'Sorry,' she found herself instantly apologising, and knew then that her heart was winning over her head.

'Consider yourself forgiven,' he said, interrupting their walking to stop and place a brief kiss on the end of her nose, setting up the most unimaginable riot inside her, before they walked on.

Not trusting herself to come back with anything, Perry stayed quiet for the next five minutes as they trudged across a field, hedgerows bursting with all manner of delights for anyone with an eye to see.

'How are you sleeping?' he asked suddenly, causing her to hope if they were to have conversation it wasn't going to be about her health, a subject she was growing weary of.

'Splendidly,' she answered, having second thoughts and thinking it a pretty innocuous subject anyway. At least she'd been able to answer his first question honestly enough.

'You haven't been troubled by nightmares since that first one?' he probed.

'No, thank goodness,' she replied, still able to recall vividly the waking part of her nightmare.

'Good,' he said, then casually, 'Still think about him?'

He meant Trevor, of course. And though she found it amazing that a couple of days could go by with Trevor never entering her mind, to have Nash thinking she was as fickle as he found the rest of womankind was something her heart didn't want.

'What do you think?' she parried—and saw he didn't think a great deal of her answer.

'I think you're a fool to give him another moment's thought,' he said roughly, and let go her arm as they came to a gate. He made no move to open the gate, however, but rested his elbow on the top and turned to look at her, his grey eyes narrowed so that she wondered what else was coming.

'This other man—the man you loved before Coleman. What happened to him?'

'Other man?' she exclaimed, usually just about able to keep up with him, but this time finding he had lost her.

'The man you must have loved more, by the sound of it,' Nash elucidated, his grey eyes steady on hers. 'Coleman said you hadn't been to bed with him but that there'd been someone else before him.'

Straightaway then Perry recalled Trevor's assumption that with her being married, it naturally followed ... 'Er—there wasn't—er—hasn't been anybody,' she stammered, not comfortable with the direction the conversation was taking.

She saw Nash didn't believe her before he turned some of the contempt so far reserved for Trevor her way. 'I thought you'd grown out of the habit of trying to pull the wool over my eyes,' he said cuttingly, and turned abruptly away to unlatch the gate so they should walk through.

But anger at having her honesty questioned had sent

her embarrassment fleeing. 'I'm not telling lies!' erupted from her as she refused to move a step. And, made angrier still that when Nash turned and his watching eyes were showing he still didn't believe her, 'Trevor Coleman's only foundation for thinking I'd had a . . .' she faltered at what she was about to say, but was too furious not to finish it, '. . . a lover was the fact he discovered about me being married.' She saw Nash's eyebrows shoot up as he got there before her clearer explanation came. 'He thought—thinks—must have done, that our marriage was a—normal one.' Fed up suddenly, she presented him with her back, not sure she wanted to carry on with their walk.

In two minds about marching off and leaving him, suddenly, she felt a hand come down on either shoulder and felt Nash turning her to face him. With hostile eyes she looked up—then all hostility vanished.

Somehow, whether by weighing up what he so far knew about her, or by just plainly believing what she said, she didn't know, but somehow doubt was going from him and incredulity grew in its place.

'You mean . . .' he began. Then, all doubt gone, 'Oh, my . . .' he began, but didn't finish that either as he took her in his arms, his head drawing nearer. And it was another world to her to feel the warm gentle touch of his mouth on hers.

It had meant to be a kiss of apology, she knew, but the chemistry in her that had a habit of over-reacting when Nash kissed her had her arms going up and around him, so that although he pulled his head back to look at her, the invitation on her sweet face was replied to.

His mouth on hers again, the pressure firming, her body pulled closer up against his, had her responding wildly. She felt his hands beneath her jacket pulling her closer still, and moaned softly from the sheer pleasure such closeness with him gave. She knew then as his lips left her to stray to her throat that whatever he asked of her she would give, willingly.

'Oh, Nash,' she groaned, unable to save herself, and felt his mouth quieting hers as his hands caressed from the back of her to the front, every caressing movement causing a shiver of delight to take her.

That was until she heard him murmur, 'I'm not sure you're up to this.' And then she cared not that his concern for her welfare had made him wonder if she was fit enough to be made complete love to. She saw only that even while she could tell he desired her, Nash Devereux would never let himself be so far gone in any situation that he failed to think with cold clarity.

Angry, with herself more than him, she later thought, that while his brain had still been ticking over she hadn't been thinking at all, she jerked out of his arms.

'Good heavens, Nash,' thank God for pride, 'you really didn't think I intended to go *all* the way, did you?' She didn't like the way his eyes were narrowing, but managed to find something that would do for a light scornful laugh as she reminded him, 'Haven't I only just told you . . .' flying into her head came the words he had once used, 'I'm a good girl, I am?'

Her scorn had pricked him, she saw that as he stared grimly at her. 'So you say,' he said derisively, 'but I hope you won't think me too much of a cad,' his tone was hard as he bit out, 'if I remark on the bloody good imitation you gave that you weren't.'

Perry was haring off across the field as his, 'Walk, don't run,' was bellowed after her. And she wanted to scream, 'Go to hell!' because, even furious with her as he was—no doubt because this time it had been she who had halted their lovemaking before that divorce was made 'the harder to come by'—that hard calculating part of him could remember she had been injured and was not up to tackling a sprint yet.

She was out of breath when she reached the house and leaned on the hall table to catch her breath, the telephone it housed making her jump when it suddenly shrilled. She ignored it, her temper gone, ready to cry at what Nash could so effortlessly do to her.

But the phone didn't stop ringing. It forced her to forget her feelings as she realised that with Bert most likely still outside servicing his car, and Ellie taking the opportunity of putting her feet up this Sunday afternoon, it was left to her to answer it.

She picked up the instrument, spotted a telephone pad and a pencil and was ready to take a message as she read out the number from off the dial.

'Put Nash on, will you,' ordered a bossy female voice, sending darts of jealousy spearing.

'He's not in,' Perry said more sharply than she meant, though whoever it was at the other end didn't deserve any better if she thought this was the way to talk to Nash's hired help.

'Who *is* that?' The voice had sharpened too, firing Perry's wilting spirit.

With the greatest of pleasure she delivered, 'Mrs Nash Devereux—may I ask who *you* are?'

Moments of silence were her answer. Then the voice altered, and a bitchiness came through. 'So it's *your* turn to be installed at Greenfields, is it?' Jealousy wasn't limited to darts as great shafts of that emotion took Perry at the implication that whoever the woman at the other end was, she had once been installed in Nash's home. Wanting badly to slam down the phone, Perry found just sufficient control to hang on, and heard a tinkly laugh followed by, 'Make the most of it, my dear—I assure you it won't be for long. Tell Nash Elvira rang . . .'

Perry didn't wait to hear what else Elvira Newman had to say. Just hearing her name, recalling the beauty photographed with Nash at the airport, was enough to lose the scant control she had. The phone was banged down and she was in her room before she remembered Nash had told her he hadn't wanted to be met at the airport by the press—or anyone.

That should have made her feel better, but with the realisation she could no longer avoid facing—her jealousy, the way she couldn't help by respond to him just two pointers—that she had passed the stage where she thought she might be falling in love with Nash. She *was* in love with him, and there was no 'might be' about it.

Knowing full well if she followed her inclination and didn't go down to dinner he would see it as his duty to come up to enquire if her dash back to the house had exhausted her, Perry joined Nash downstairs with only a minute to spare before mealtime.

Oh, to have a fraction of his sophistication, she thought, that his anger with her gone he didn't bat an eyelid when referring to her racing away from him and hoping she suffered no ill effects.

'I'm fine,' she said quietly, and took her place at the table.

There were many times as dinner progressed when Nash said something that at any other time would have had her lips twitching, or even laughing outright. But Elvira Newman's intimation that she had once been installed in Nash's home, without question as his mistress, just wouldn't stop gnawing away at her.

'Your attempt to be athlete of the year has taken more out of you than you're admitting,' he said suddenly, causing Perry, who had been staring into her coffee cup, to realise he had been closely observing her while she had been picking at her meal. 'You've barely eaten anything. You'd better have an early night.'

About to snap 'Yes, doctor,' she felt pain that he was clearly saying he'd had enough of her company. 'What a good idea,' she said, her pain giving her tongue a sarcastic edge.

Ignoring that his eyes were starting to glint, she picked up her cup intending to drain it and go. Then realised she would have to tell him about the telephone call, that or have his smart brain wondering why she hadn't when he found out, as he surely would the next time he saw Elvira Newman.

'By the way, I've just remembered,' she said without blinking, 'Elvira Newman rang.'

She wished she knew what he was thinking. She was aware his eyes were upon her, and avoided looking at him by taking several sips of her coffee. Then she heard him casually ask:

'Did she say what she wanted?'

'I have no idea.' Perry placed her cup in its saucer, a knife turning inside, and her hurt wouldn't be held in any longer. 'Apart from charmingly remarking on its being *my* turn to be installed, and telling me it wouldn't be for long, she had little else to say.'

As soon as she had repeated the bitchy remarks she wished she hadn't. But it was too late then in the lengthening pause to pull them back. And then Nash was causing her agonies that he had immediately guessed at her jealousy.

'So that's what's been niggling away at you.' About to hotly deny it, Perry was awash with relief when she heard the different construction he had for the solemn dinner partner she had been. 'Your good-girl morality objects strongly to anyone thinking you're here as my mistress.'

'I told her I was your wife—well, that I was Mrs Nash Devereux,' she said, and could have groaned out loud that she had just cut her own throat by sweeping away the excuse he had handed her for being unsmiling throughout dinner. 'Well, she asked who I was,' she added, just in case Nash thought she had adopted proprietorial rights and volunteered the information.

'So you put her right on that score,' he said, and she could almost hear him crossing off one of his conclusions. 'So what is it that's upset you, Perry?' And he crossed off another. 'It can't be because I kissed you, you had the last laugh there.' Her eyes shot to him to hear him admit he hadn't liked it when she had broken away from him.

She couldn't hold his look; she wished he would leave it alone. About to follow up his suggestion that she had an early night, say that she was tired, anything, anything rather than have him discerning that for the first time in her life jealousy was plaguing her, she opened her mouth to plead tiredness and found Nash there before her with fresh calculations.

'It *is* your sense of morality, as I first thought, isn't it?' And suddenly his voice was a shade kinder. 'Does it offend your sense of decency that I might have installed Elvira here for the purpose of . . .'

'No. No, of course not,' she butted in quickly before her plain-speaking husband could finish. 'Good grief, Nash, you may have discovered that I . . .' She wished she hadn't interrupted, and couldn't finish the sentence.

'That you don't—indulge,' he finished it for her, and she hurriedly took over again.

'But that isn't to say that I'm entirely unaware of what goes on around me.' She found, regardless of what she said, that he still thought her sense of morality had been offended.

'Would it make you feel better,' he said kindly, 'if I told you Elvira Newman has never been here?'

It did. Perry's heart began to sing again. But she wasn't going to make the mistake of looking at him so he could see how his words affected her. She pushed her coffee cup away and stood up, now ready to leave, fighting all she could for a touch of his sophistication so he shouldn't know God was in her heaven, for the moment, and all was right with her world.

'Good heavens, Nash,' she said, making for the door and finding he was there to open it for her, 'it doesn't bother me in the slightest who you have here—I won't be here much longer myself, will I?'

Oh, how she wished, as she lay in bed that night praying for sleep, that she hadn't needled him with her lofty attitude.

'That's true,' he had agreed, 'you won't.' And as though he couldn't wait for the day she would be fit enough to leave—sounding a death knoll to any foolish hopes her ridiculous heart might have thought to nurse—he told her bluntly, 'There's no room in my life for permanent—arrangements.'

Having spent a night wrestling with her pride, Perry rose early the next morning, fully determined Nash was going to take her back to London when he went. But she was to find that, as early as she had arisen, Nash was an earlier bird—he had already left when she went downstairs looking for him.

Disgruntled at experiencing a twinge of relief at the chance to spend another day in his home, to be able to see and touch things he knew, she hardened her heart, making up her mind that even if it meant camping out in his car all night, Nash was going to take her with him when he left tomorrow morning.

But that plan too was doomed to failure. For Nash didn't come home that night. Nor did he come home any of the following three nights.

'He's busy, I expect,' Ellie thought she was consoling when dinner was finished on Thursday evening and still no sign of him.

Poor Ellie, Perry couldn't help thinking. Ellie had set her heart on the reconciliation and must now be wondering what on earth Nash was playing at. Especially since last week, regardless of his work load, he had returned each night.

'I expect he is,' she answered, knowing that, pressure of work or not, the reason Nash wasn't putting in an appearance at Greenfields was because she was there. And that, she found, was something she just couldn't live with.

Straightaway after breakfast the next morning she asked Ellie where Bert was, and at her enquiring look, had to tell her, 'I wondered if he'd give me a lift to the station.'

'Oh, Perry,' cried Ellie, 'Nash will be home tonight, I feel sure.'

Perry was sure he wouldn't be, nor any time while she was still there. 'He won't,' she said with conviction, and saw Ellie's loyalty to Nash was being put under a great strain as clearly she only just bit back some disapproving remark about her master's cavalier behaviour.

'Don't go by train,' Ellie urged, her loyalty to Nash winning the day. 'I don't think you realise how ill you've been, and a train journey, bundling your case with you, will undo all the healing work of the past fortnight.'

About to say she felt returned to full health—which was true—for her sins, Perry couldn't resist the appeal of Ellie's persuasions as she quickly pressed.

'Look, Bert is going to London tomorrow. Why not go with him?' and, warming to the idea, 'Another day won't hurt, surely, and Bert can take you right to your door with your case.'

It sounded common sense, Perry thought, weakening. Her pride could still be salved without depriving herself of another day in Nash's home.

'All right,' she conceded, and saw Ellie was all smiles again as she told her Bert would be leaving at nine sharp, and she'd let him know to expect a passenger.

Perry spent the day taking a last look round, standing for long moments mentally photographing everything in her mind. Her heart sore that any future dealing she had with Nash would be dealt with through the auspices of her solicitor. His absence this week, without his cutting remark of having no room in his life for permanent arrangements, had shown that if she was ever to try and get on top of the love she had for him, then she had to make a clean break, go ahead with the divorce and sever that tie with him.

But as she came into the house from the rear about six that evening, her conviction that she would never see Nash again disintegrated into nothing. For there he was coming in through the front door, dark business suit, briefcase in hand, car coat flung carelessly over his arm, tall, virile, and her heart pumping wildly, so wonderful to see.

Controlling her lips, the smile that wanted to break out like a burst of sunlight, Perry looked anywhere but at him as she approached the foot of the stairs, arriving there at the same time as him.

'Hello, stranger,' she remarked, so casually that she had to think herself there must be some brilliant actress buried deep inside her somewhere.

Nash's hand on her shoulder stayed her when she would have started up the stairs. 'Miss me?' he enquired, his manner easy as he looked down into her face, checking to see if she had improved, she guessed.

'About the same as you've missed me, I should imagine,' she avoided the question. 'And in answer to your next query, I'm hale and hearty and . . .' her voice wavered as his arm came about her shoulders as he began to climb the stairs beside her, 'and ready to go back to work,' she managed to finish, knowing her breathlessness in mounting the stairs had nothing at all to do with the physical effort involved.

They had reached the top before Nash commented, 'You are, are you?'

She nodded, unable to resist a quick look at his face. 'I—we didn't think we'd see you before I left—I'm going home tomorrow.' She saw thunder in the way his look instantly darkened, and went on hurriedly, 'B-Bert's giving me a lift. S-so I'm glad you've come home. I shouldn't like to have gone without—without thanking you for all . . .'

'You can thank me at dinner,' he bit abruptly, and left her standing.

Well! Stupefied, Perry stared after him, wondering how it was possible, after five days of longing to see him, that within the space of three minutes of doing just that he had her growing angry with him. Did he have to be so rude, so taciturn?

When Perry went down to dinner, ready to ignore him if he treated her so abruptly again, she discovered Nash was in a much more agreeable mood.

'Sherry?' he offered, his eyes on her in the brown velvet dress he had thought to pack for her. And handing her the small glass she had requested, 'May I be permitted to say how beautiful you are?'

Smitten by shyness suddenly, she couldn't handle the unexpected compliment. 'It's the dress that does it,' she said, and saw with pleasure going out of all proportion the way he smiled and shook his head as if to say her dress had nothing to do with it. He then told her how much he liked her dress, which again pleased her, making her glad he didn't think, as Trevor had done, that it made her appear remote. Then she heard him ask:

'But it isn't one you made yourself, is it?'

'I did, actually,' she said, and realised then that if she grew any more pleased at his remarks, he was very shortly going to guess how completely ready to melt she was from any kind word he tossed her way.

'How's business?' she enquired, swiftly turning the subject to matters that stood no chance of a comeback remark that would have her ready to let him walk all over her.

The corners of his mouth turned endearingly upwards. 'I should worry,' he said, his smile becoming a grin. 'With the wife I have the Corporation could fold tomorrow and I wouldn't have to wonder where my next shirt was coming from.'

The glow he caused in her by referring to her as his wife stayed with Perry as they went into the dining room. And with Nash being at his most charming, as second course followed first course, she became enchanted.

But it was when Ellie came in to serve the last course, looking moist-eyed at her as she observed how perfectly they were getting on, the harmonious atmosphere, that she shook Perry into realising the reconciliation Ellie thought Nash wanted, must from where she was standing look a certainty. It was then that Perry fell crashing back to earth.

'I'm pleased to see you're looking much better than you did a week ago,' Nash commented as Ellie closed the door on her way out.

'I'm completely recovered,' Perry answered, the glow in her gone leaving her feeling flat. She forced a bright smile. 'That's why after tomorrow you won't have to put up with me any more. Thank you so much, Nash . . .' she began to trot out.

'What's the sudden hurry to get back to London?'

His abrupt question, his chopping her off before she could finish, charm gone, had her knowing he didn't want her thanks, and didn't like either that she was now well enough to make her own decisions.

'It's where I live,' she said, not wanting to argue with him, not now, not on her last night in his home. 'It's where I work.'

'You're not fit to go back to work,' he said shortly, astounding her, for only seconds ago he had been commenting on how well she was looking.

'Yes, I am,' she argued, for all an argument was the last thing she wanted.

'Is it because of Coleman you want to go back?' he asked harshly.

Trevor! What had he got to do with anything? Perry's lips firmed that Nash could think she still hankered after Trevor after what he had done.

'It's none of your business,' she snapped rudely, and saw straightaway as his eyes glinted that he didn't care a whole heap for her speaking to him that way.

'I'm making it my business,' he told her grimly. 'He isn't the man for you, so you can put all ideas of marrying him out of your head. I'm not divorcing you, so you can . . .'

'*You're* not divorcing *me*!'

Suddenly there was spirit firing up in her. Spirit given a boost by the pain of knowing Nash didn't want her himself—didn't want her, yet thought he had an entitlement to discard or approve any man who did. The pain in her knew no rationalisation as, on her feet, her voice rising—either that or break down and weep at the rejection she felt—she yelled:

'*You* don't hold the option!' And in her hurt not above throwing in a red herring, 'With Trevor and his mother knowing about my marriage I have no need to worry about any publicity ensuing from our divorce!'

She broke off as his eyes glittered dangerously, then backed to the door as he too stood. She knew tears weren't very far away and, afraid he might hold her there, yanked open the door and, in defiance before tears, delivered her parting salvo.

'I'm not waiting for you to divorce me, Nash Devereux. I shall see my solicitor about an annulment on Monday!'

She had been weeping on and off for a full five minutes when the sound of male footsteps halting outside her bedroom door had the tears promptly ceasing.

Hastily she brushed the dampness from her eyes, then stared fascinated, her heart thumping crazily, as the door handle turned. She watched, her eyes going wide, as Nash stepped into her room.

'What . . .' was all she managed to choke, her thoughts chaotic at the purposeful way he closed the door behind him.

'You've been crying,' were the first words he spoke. And as he came nearer Perry had to fight as hard as she could against the vulnerability she was feeling.

'I can cry if I w-want to.'

'Why should you want to?' There was a tenderness in

his tone, and when she couldn't or wouldn't answer, he leaned forward and placed a kiss that was a caress on both her eyes.

'Nash, I . . .' she tried, for already her bones were traitorously ready to melt. She tried with all she had left to get herself together, and asked, hoping for a coldness that just wasn't there, 'What do you want, Nash?'

'I don't want you to cry any more,' he said softly, his hands coming to her shoulders, imperceptibly drawing her closer. Lightly his mouth came to whisper a kiss across hers, firing in her that same old instant response. 'Your eyes are too beautiful to know the sadness of tears,' he said gently, and there was there in his voice a sensitivity to her distress that when he went to kiss her lightly again, Perry found herself meeting him half way.

'Nash.' She whispered his name without knowing why, but felt no panic as lightly once more he kissed her.

Reason told her she had no need to panic. Nash had always been ruled by his head. He kissed her again, and wanting, needing his kisses, she couldn't help but listen to the voice that urged why shouldn't she have them. He wouldn't let it go too far, she could be certain of that. Hadn't she had proof of that in the past?

'My beautiful Perry,' he breathed, his face not smiling as his eyes devoured her face, his glance going from her mouth to her eyes and to her lips again.

And it was then she gave herself up to the heady delight of his kisses, knowing that at whatever point he chose to break off his lovemaking she would have this rapturous feeling he aroused to remember—for break off he would.

In the circle of his arms she stood returning his kisses without reservation, hungry to be held by him, to be kissed, to kiss back. His hands caressed her, but as she knew he wouldn't, he made no move to take her nearer to the bed. Minutes of giving and taking slipped by in his arms as he awakened a need in her for more, yet more.

But colour flooded her face when his hands came to her zip and her dress fell to the floor. Her eyes met his, and she knew he had observed her flushed cheeks, when with his mouth curving softly, he asked:

'Would you feel better if I put out the light?'

Perry nodded, feeling cold in the moments he was away, and then hot all over, when he had her in his arms once more, to find he had shed his jacket.

His hands pressed her to him, her thin covering no covering at all with their bodies so close. 'Oh, Nash,' she cried, when he undid her bra and disposed of it, his hands coming to cup her breasts, his lips on the hardened crowns making her clutch on to him.

And it was then, when she heard Nash groan too, that, as she was half delirious from his lovemaking, the thought fluttered in that perhaps he did not intend leaving.

She did not want him to leave as once more he pressed her to him, her love-swollen breasts meeting his warm hair-roughened chest, having no idea when he had removed his shirt; it was then something inside her wanted to hold back.

'Nash!' she gasped, only to realise he was able to cope with this last-minute backing away.

'It's all right, my love,' he gentled her, that "my love" enough to have her all his again. 'It's natural for you to be scared the first time—just trust me.'

She did trust him. 'Oh, Nash, Nash!' she cried, comprehending only that he understood, no thought given that it didn't sound as though his hard-headed reason was going to get a hearing.

When he picked her up in his arms and carried her to the bed, taking his arms from her briefly, Perry knew only a fevered longing to have his arms about her again.

'My love,' he breathed, then he was lying with her, was naked, and so understanding of her shyness, she was able to deny him nothing.

CHAPTER ELEVEN

PERRY slept late, then stirred in her sleep, remembrance filtering through as she surfaced and was suddenly wide awake. With a half-smile on her lips she turned tentatively—and her smile died. Nash wasn't there.

For several unnumbered minutes she was happy. Even without Nash beside her her heart raced excitedly as she recalled that beautiful togetherness they had shared, the way he had overcome her shyness, succeeded so gently, so unhurriedly, in drawing from her a passion new to her.

They were sublime minutes for her, recapturing how without words she had given over her love. And then the gentle smile of remembrance began to fade, edged out by insecure wonderings of—had it been so marvellous for Nash too?

Insecurity grew, nurtured by memory of the beautiful, sophisticated women she had seen photographed with him. Women who knew what it was all about. And with that insecurity crept in the question—why?

Why had Nash lost his head last night? Why, when previously that cold clinical logic of his had stopped him? Last night she had looked very little different from that first time at her flat. She had even been wearing the same dress. Insecurity, doubt, mingled with her own logic, cold too in the light of day. And the unwanted thought could not be avoided—had he lost his head at all?

A sickness invaded her, and suddenly she was out of bed, bathing, dressing, all in record time, as she tried to evade her thoughts. But unwanted thoughts followed every action.

There was no way of evading them. No way she could avoid remembering the way she had rushed from the dining room in fear Nash would see her in tears. But her thinking had been clear when she had told him she was going to see about an annulment on Monday.

Feeling winded, just as though she had received a body blow as the nightmare thought struck forcibly home, Perry clutched at her stomach. Had he deliberately made love to her in order to take away any chance of her getting that annulment?

Nash was a man who liked to make the decisions, she knew that. And she saw then, too late, that she had angered him by saying she was going to see about an annulment on Monday.

A dry choking sound left her as she realised that what last night had been all about was that Nash objected to being dictated to by a woman. It had been the simplest thing in the world to take from her the chance of getting the marriage annulment she had so defiantly let him know she considered her right!

Not wanting to believe he had coldbloodedly, deliberately set about making love to her, she sank down on the bed, a cynicism entering her heart as she wondered what made her think she was different from any of the dozens of women he must have known.

Dispiritedly, but now coldly angry, she eventually left her room ready with a few short sharp words should Nash wander out of his study.

'Morning, Perry.'

She turned to see Ellie coming from the kitchen area. 'Morning, Ellie,' from somewhere near the bottom of her boots she drummed up a smile.

'Lovely day again,' Ellie said cheerfully. 'Ready for breakfast?'

The thought of breakfast made Perry's stomach heave. 'Just coffee,' she answered. And because the question wouldn't stay down, 'Nash has had his breakfast, I suppose?'

'Ate heartily,' Ellie said with her usual smile. 'You've just missed him.'

'He's—er—gone out?'

Perry didn't know how she kept her face from crumpling, her last hope that she had got it all wrong dying, as Ellie confirmed he had. It just showed how much he cared.

'Gone clay pigeon shooting, I expect. He does occasionally when he's home Saturdays. He . . .'

But Perry had heard enough. 'Bert hasn't gone yet, has he?' she asked, taking a speedy look at her watch to see it said a quarter past nine.

Ellie's look was suspicious as she told her, 'He's later than he meant to be—he's just getting the car out . . .' Perry headed for the stairs in a hurry, Ellie's, 'What . . .' following her.

'Tell him to hang on for me,' she called back and, not waiting to hear what Ellie had to say in answer to that, charged up to her room, collected the case she had packed yesterday, ignoring the brown velvet dress Nash had draped over a chair—she would never wear it again, Ellie could throw it away for all she cared—and was running downstairs terrified in case Ellie had not asked Bert to wait.

She found both Bert and Ellie in the rear courtyard, Ellie looking so worried and disturbed that Perry put her arms round the housekeeper's wiry frame and hugged her. 'Goodbye, Ellie,' she said, and didn't dare look at her as she clambered into the car in case she relayed to Nash she had looked on the verge of tears.

'What shall I tell Nash?' Ellie's bewildered-sounding voice reached her.

'He won't expect me to be here when he gets back,' she told her, and was hard pressed not to break down at the truth of that as Bert, already later than he had meant to be, set the A40 in motion.

How could she have stayed, she wondered, knowing hurt as it did, she was taking the only way open to her? Nash hadn't asked her to stay when she had told him she was leaving; he would expect her to be gone when he came back from his clay pigeon shooting. A fine fool she would have made of herself had she stayed! She could imagine the surprise on his face, the 'I thought you were going with Bert this morning' look. What would she have felt like then—the dejection she felt now added to? Her pride would have never again surfaced.

'You never did get round to explaining the intricacies of model railways, Bert,' she said, turning to him, needing to get away and quickly from her thoughts, and for most of the drive had Bert eulogising on his favourite subject.

They were nearly in London when one of the tyres punctured, a circumstance he hadn't allowed time for as he got the spare from the boot. Aware that he had been over fifteen minutes later setting off than he had intended and was anxious not to be late in picking up his friend, Perry waited only until they were on their way again to tell him:

'No need to take me to my door, Bert, it's too far out of your way.'

And when he wouldn't hear of it she insisted that she could easily get a taxi. But she still had to work on him for another ten minutes before he finally gave in.

Once she had waved goodbye, wishing Bert a good time at his exhibition, she was in no hurry to get to her flat. Her suitcase was a nuisance, of course, but what was there to hurry home for? She had today and tomorrow to get through before she went to work on Monday—two days of probably sitting in her flat with only herself and thoughts she didn't want for company.

She walked around until she found a café, spending pensive moments over coffee, then another coffee. Then a feeling of being stifled by her thoughts had her going outside, but still not wanting to go home. It was a real effort of will not to weep right there on the pavement as the thought struck that she didn't want to return to her flat because it didn't seem like home any more. Greenfields, where Nash was, was home.

In between resting her case she walked on, trying to come to terms with her empty future. She knew then that she was solving nothing by not wanting to return to her flat. She had some material there, she remembered, trying to turn her thoughts into other channels, so she could spend the weekend making something up. Never less enthusiastic, she had the luck at that moment to see a cruising taxi with its flag up.

Sitting unhappily in the back of the cab, she composed herself to greet Mrs Foster. She would be pleased to see her, Perry knew that. And she'd have to look pleased to be back—but she wasn't. Yet she hadn't any choice.

'Here we are, love.'

Settling with the driver, Perry turned to hoist up her case from where he had set it down on the pavement. Then she blinked, and for one crazy moment thought she had gone off her head. For that was Nash's car parked outside Mrs Foster's, she was sure of it!

But it couldn't be—he was off clay pigeon shooting somewhere! Don't be ridiculous, she steadied her palpitating heart. She didn't know his car number and there must be half a dozen cars that looked like his.

She inserted her key in the front door, her heart resuming its dull beat. Was this how it was going to be? she wondered, turning to close the door. Everywhere she went something to remind her of him? She sighed. Better tap on Mrs Foster's door before she went up.

A sound of movement behind her told her a tap on Mrs Foster's door wasn't necessary. She turned, a smile ready for her landlady, then her smile froze, her heart turned giddy again. It wasn't Mrs Foster who stood there tall and straight. It was Nash!!

'You're clay pigeon shooting,' she gasped idiotically. Then all that lay between them scattered all thought as a furious blush stained every visible part of her, memories crowding in, of his kisses tender on her skin, of not so long ago lying naked in his arms.

She saw the smile that came to him as he observed her scarlet colour, but she found relief from embarrassment in hearing Mrs Foster limping to her door, and was glad of somewhere else to look.

'Hello, Perry love,' Mrs Foster greeted her from her doorway. 'Oh, you do look better. You were such a poorly-looking girl when Mr Devereux took you away.'

Perry went over to her, hoping her colour was more normal as she greeted her landlady, ignoring the clamour in her heart region, the one thought only going round in her brain—What in heaven's name was Nash doing here?

Then she heard him too speaking to her landlady, charm and sincerity there as he thanked her for the coffee she must have given him, adding to her disbelieving ears:

'We'll call in and see you before we go.'

We go! Wide-eyed, she stared at him, but without looking at her he had his hand beneath her elbow and was urging her towards the stairs.

Stubbornly she refused to budge. 'What's . . .' going on, she would have said had she the chance.

'Come on, darling,' he said smoothly, 'we don't want to keep Mrs Foster standing about, do we?'

Darling! Utterly confused, Perry turned to Mrs Foster for guidance. 'I'll see you when you come down,' Mrs Foster told her, and mysteriously, 'I'm going to miss you, Perry.' Then she started to retreat inside her own apartments, leaving Perry open-mouthed. And whether she liked it or not she found she was being propelled up the stairs, her feet moving despite her determination not to budge an inch.

When they reached her flat the door being ajar told her Nash had borrowed the spare key from her landlady. That

in itself was sufficient cheek. But when reluctantly she
went into her sitting room, she was staggered to see her
spare suitcase and numerous cardboard boxes had been
packed with all her personal possessions.

'What . . .' she gasped, turning to a steady-eyed Nash,
anger flaring that it looked as though she was being
evicted, and it just had to have something to do with <u>him</u>.
'What the hell is going on?'

It had been expecting to much to expect the Nash
Devereux she knew to ever look ashamed. He didn't now,
as casually, or so it seemed to her, he leaned up against
the doorway and remarked:

'I thought it might save time if I started your packing
for you.'

'Packing!'

'I'd like to get back to Greenfields in time for lunch if
we can.' And as cool as you like, 'Ellie said she would
prepare something extra special for you.'

'Look here, Nash Devereux,' Perry exploded, beginning
to see a chink of light, 'I'm going nowhere with you,
Greenfields or—or anywhere else!' God, didn't he know
how he was hurting her? One night in bed with her and
he fancied keeping it up for a week or two, not much
longer, she would bet on it. Anger spurted again. 'And . . .
and I think you're the vilest creature imaginable that you
know so little of me you think I would be agreeable to
such an arrangement!'

That shook him, she thought with satisfaction. She could
see it had in the way he straightened from the door, that
casual look leaving him. She even thought he had lost a
little of his colour.

'You mean you're—not agreeable? His voice had a
hoarse ring to it, but she wasn't fooled. He might desire
her now—for a short while—she reminded herself, feeling a
weakness of wanting to be in his arms, but not for very long.

'No, I am not,' she said shortly, ignoring an inner voice
that tried to tell her she was mad to think of forgoing a

few weeks of love with him. 'And—I think it's despicable of you to suggest such a thing!' Anger started to fade as another moment of wanting to give in took her, and she knew then she had to fight him all the way, oppose him, for if she didn't she might find herself giving in. Weakness was controlled, anger she needed there again to help her. 'You've got the wrong girl, Nash,' she said heatedly. 'Last—last night I let—let you get to me. But,' her voice that had gone shaky, strengthened, 'But you know better than most that I've never gone in for—temporary arrangements.' She saw his brow clear, and wanted to hit him as his mouth began to curve as the words, 'I don't intend starting now,' left her.

'Who told you it would be a temporary arrangement?' he had the nerve to ask.

Open-mouthed, in no way believing he had suddenly decided to change his life style, Perry reminded him. 'You did. That afternoon—evening, after Elvira Newman phoned. You said then . . .'

She didn't need to remind him, he had instant recall.

'I've said a lot of things,' he told her, coming away from the door, his approach having her backing away, afraid of that magic in his touch. 'Too many damn things, in my fight against the power of you.'

'Power of me?'

She stood rooted as he neared her, felt that thrilling tingle shoot through her when he took hold of her by her upper arms. 'You've known from that first evening, the evening we came here after dining out, that I desired you.'

Yes, she knew that. It had been a mutual desiring, she hadn't been able to stop herself anyway. 'But not enough to have you ignoring that cold logic you have in your brain that told you you would mess up the divorce if you heeded that desire,' she said, pulling out of his grip and backing away again while she still could.

This time Nash didn't follow her, but stood watching her as he admitted the truth of what she was saying. 'I can't deny it,' he agreed. 'Marriage was something I'd avoided like the plague—a proper marriage, that is—so I got out.'

'Kiss and run,' she inserted, bitterness welling up inside that if she went with him, he wouldn't regard her as a proper wife—she would be his mistress for a short time, that was all.

'If you like,' he said, his eyes still on her. Then he proceeded to shatter her by stating, 'But when I went to bed that night and couldn't get to sleep for thinking about you, I knew you could if I didn't watch it, start to get under my skin.'

'Under . . .' she gaped, never expecting to hear him admit such a thing.

'That's why I agreed to the divorce,' he went on to tell her. And, never one for hiding in corners, 'I wanted you out of my life—out of my head.'

Perry wondered why her heart wouldn't behave when all he was saying was that if under his skin she was, then the quickest way to get her out was to have her living with him. For it was as clear as day that once she was from under his skin, his desire sated, she could go, and he would carry on the way he had always done.

'So you thought by arranging for me to see Mr Leighton I would soon be out of your life. How dreadful of me to go and have an accident!' Sarcasm came to assist, but it didn't make her feel any better. 'A pity for you I had the certificate of marriage copy with me, wasn't it?'

'I'm not sure,' he said, when she had been positive he was always sure of everything.

Her mouth firmed as she took that to indicate that he wasn't sure yet whether she was going with him or not. Then she felt her heart give another wild surge of hope as Nash added:

'It wasn't until I saw you in hospital, unconscious to the world, that I had to face the fact that what I'd been telling myself was untrue. It wasn't just desire for your body I felt. It hurt me that you were hurt.'

That he should ever know pain on her account had her

own feelings, the ache in her heart, promptly and completely disregarded. And there was a softness entering her voice as regretfully she said:

'Oh, Nash!'

It was all the invitation he needed. In a few strides he was with her, looking down into her face as his arms wrapped loosely round her.

'I began to suffer agonies on your account, my dear,' he told her gently. 'I found myself pacing the hospital corridor, and had to lecture myself sternly when you started to recover, that if I didn't watch it I would find myself in love with you.'

Her heart went leaden. He had proved before he could master his emotions. Had the love that had started to grow in him for her been rooted out before it could take a hold? She knew it had.

'It must have been most inconvenient for you to feel you had to take me into your home,' she said woodenly, and received a small shake from him that the softness in her had disappeared.

'I had no intention of leaving you where that animal Coleman could get to you again,' he told her, all his warmth going as he said it. Then as she struggled to get out of his arms, he suddenly smiled, hanging on to her as he confessed, 'Taking you to Greenfields, I soon saw, was a very big mistake.'

Perry stared at him, unable to comprehend why if it had been such a mistake he was now proposing that she should go back there with him.

'You've lost me somewhere, Nash,' she told him. 'You've not long ago stated quite clearly that you want me back there as your mistress.' She went white at the answer she received.

'Mistress *and* wife,' he said, his mouth curving again at the shock in her eyes.

Whether he thought she looked as though she would fall down if she didn't soon sit, she didn't know. But it was then that he led her over to the settee, to sit with her, to brush a stray strand of hair back from her face, as he explained,

'I didn't want to fall in love, didn't want a wife. But when I found I was tearing through my work each day so I could rush home to you, I knew I was facing the beginning of the end.'

Happiness burst in on her. She felt the end of the rainbow was hers. Happiness didn't last. Insecurity chased it away as it had when she had awakened happy that morning.

'You didn't come home at all last week,' she reminded him, trying to get her voice to rise above the flatness she was feeling so he should not know how much having his love would mean to her.

'And it was sheer hell not doing so,' he told her, which lifted her, but only briefly. 'I needed that self-inflicted punishment to make me realise what it would be like for the rest of my life if I didn't turn my back on every preconceived idea I'd ever held.'

Dully Perry realised that whatever it was he was saying he felt for her, there was no spontaneity about it. His head would always rule him. Solemnly she looked at him, and Nash, seeing the unsmiling look of her, went on, urging:

'Try to understand, Perry. From the day my mother walked out and I saw my father's utter despair I knew women could hurt if you let them get to you. I was fourteen and already wary of women when my father at last picked himself up and started to bring home one good-time girl after another. By the time I was twenty I knew marriage I could do without. The experience with Lydia cemented that opinion.'

Perry wanted to interrupt him then to say that she did understand. How could she not with the example of her sex that had been thrust before him at a very tender age? She wanted to tell him that all women were not like the women he had known, but had little faith he would believe her.

'I considered myself a confirmed bachelor,' he went on when no smile or word came from her. 'It was no part of my plan to have you in my system . . .'

She did interrupt him then, finding her voice to say, 'Was it p-part of your plan to come home last night and . . .' she nearly said seduce me, but if it had been seduction then he hadn't had any opposition, had he, 'and get me into bed with you?' she asked. Hurrying on when she received a dark look for what she was saying, 'I mean— well, if you wanted to get me out of your system . . .'

Heart-searing thoughts were recalled. Painful, bitter thoughts of how it had been Nash's cold determination to be the one to take the decision when their marriage should be terminated that had brought him to her room, and she rushed on before he could speak:

'You made sure an annulment was out of the question, didn't you?' she said, anger coming from her raw hurt. 'It was something the great Nash Devereux couldn't allow, wasn't it, that some woman should turn around and tell him what she was going to do about—about an—an entanglement he was part of.'

She ran out of steam as Nash stared at her as though she had just stupefied him. 'My God,' he breathed, 'the nutty way your brain works! So that's why you ran out on me this morning. You thought——' he looked completely nonplussed for a couple of seconds before he got his thoughts together. 'You actually thought I came to your room, took your virginity, simply because I was piqued that I wasn't running the show?'

'Well,' she said lamely, not likely to be made to think she had been doing some idiotic thinking, for all she hoped it was true. Had being in love with Nash scrambled her otherwise fairly uncluttered thinking? And, her intelligence at work again, 'You didn't stay around to tell me otherwise, did you? Ellie said you'd probably gone . . .'

'Oh, Perry, my little love,' Nash said tenderly, 'I can see I shall have to spell it out for you, for all I thought that wonderful merging of minds, hearts and souls we shared last night said it all. Your statement that you wanted the marriage annulled threw me, I'll admit, but that wasn't why I came to your room.'

'It wasn't?'

'No, it was not,' he said unequivocally. 'I was as mad as hell after you'd gone, but as I started to cool down all I could remember was the way you looked before you so rapidly disappeared. You looked ready to break your heart,' he smiled then as he confessed. 'I found out then that whether you wanted an annulment or not, I just couldn't bear the thought of you upstairs breaking your little heart all alone. I just couldn't take it; I had to come and try to comfort you. And when I did, when I had you in my arms—well, I just lost my head.'

'You . . .' Perry felt choked, unable to go on. Nash, the man she had always thought completely in control was admitting that when he had taken her in his arms and kissed her, the cold logic of his thinking had disappeared! Hope surged upward as with his arm about her he pulled her close as though never intending to let her go.

'I'm in love with you, my lovely wife,' he said, his voice thickening. 'I came home last night with every intention of telling you so. I acted like a sore-headed bear when you greeted me with the news that you were leaving—tried to redress the balance at dinner—and we both know how that ended.'

Perry found difficulty in swallowing. She stared wordlessly into warm grey eyes, unable to believe what Nash was saying, what the look on his face was saying. None of it could be happening. But it was like a symphony starting to play in her ears when Nash, seeing she was struggling, told her:

'I have fought it, I can't deny—fought hard against the love I have for you. This need for you that makes home no place unless you're there.'

'Oh, Nash,' she whispered, unbelievable happiness singing inside her.

'So please, please say you'll come back with me, because I swear there's no point in my calling any place home without you to come home to.'

Shyly, love bursting in her, showing in her eyes. Perry raised a loving hand to touch the side of his face, and saw sincerity and a deep abiding love there in his eyes for her.

'Oh, my love,' she said softly, using the words he had used when he had made love to her. 'Oh, Nash . . .'

His name died on her lips as her answer given in the way she was, he crushed her to him, his mouth devouring hers, tiny kisses covering her face, joy in him, in his pounding heart beneath her hand.

'Darling, darling girl,' he said tenderly when he pulled back so he could see into her shining eyes. 'Don't ever, ever give me a shock such as the one I received when I got back this morning.'

'You expected to find me there?' she asked huskily, her eyes feeding hungrily on his face.

'I was completely stunned that you weren't. I just couldn't believe it, not after the way we'd been together.'

'You knew I was in love with you?' she asked shyly.

'Say that again,' Nash broke off to urge. 'The last part.'

Perry smiled. 'I love you very much,' she said, her voice low, and all was silent for long moments as he drew her close again, kissing her deeply.

Love filled her flat as the kiss ended and they pulled back each to gaze at the other, until finally Perry just had to speak.

'Ellie told you Bert had given me a lift?'

He nodded, his eyes still on her as if he couldn't tear his look away. 'I couldn't believe it. For the only time in my life, I remember,' he revealed, 'I was so shattered that in jumping in my car and chasing after you I took the wrong route. By the time I'd sorted myself out and realised Bert would have gone another way I decided it would be better to come straight on here.'

'Was that when you decided to give my notice on this flat for me?' she asked, marvelling at the freedom in teasing him, seeing his unashamed grin as he answered.

'I thought I might do that as I drove along. The way we were when we were in each other's arms,' he paused to kiss her—he had to—before he continued, 'the way you'd been with me last night—You couldn't not love me, I thought, not and be so shyly willing to let me have your innocence.'

Perry's face went a delightful pink. 'My darling! My beautiful shy love,' Nash murmured, and kissed her. She felt that her heart was pounding too as his hand covered it. 'My wife,' he said, the way he said it, satisfaction, undisguised happiness there, having her thrilling anew.

Then as though the words 'my wife' had reminded him of something, his eyes never leaving her face, he said softly:

'You haven't asked me where I went this morning, what it was that had me tearing myself from my adorable bride. What it was that had me fighting an inner battle not to stay and kiss you awake.'

'You didn't go clay pigeon shooting?' she asked, knowing suddenly his errand had been much more important than that.

For answer Nash dipped his hand into his pocket and withdrew a small square box. 'I went to buy this. It mattered to me—I was hoping it mattered to you.'

Perry couldn't stop the tears that rushed to her eyes when he pulled back the lid from the box and she saw what it contained. It was a wedding ring.

'You said you'd thrown the other one in the river,' he said softly, taking her left hand in his. Then, his voice stronger, sincere and loving, gently he slid the plain gold band over her wedding finger, saying as he did so, keeping hold of it when it was home, 'With this ring I thee wed. With my body I thee worship.'

Tears were streaming down Perry's face as Nash came to the end. 'I love you, my darling wife,' he murmured tenderly, wiping away her tears as reverently he kissed her. Then, still in that quiet loving way, he kissed her wedding ring, kissed her hand.

'Let's go home, my dear, dear love,' he said.

ROMANCE

Variety is the spice of romance

Each month, Mills & Boon publish new romances. New stories about people falling in love. A world of variety in romance – from the best writers in the romantic world. Choose from these titles in September.

THE LION OF LA ROCHE   Yvonne Whittal
SATAN'S MASTER   Carole Mortimer
ILLUSION   Charlotte Lamb
SUBSTITUTE BRIDE   Margaret Pargeter
UNTOUCHED WIFE   Rachel Lindsay
INNOCENT OBSESSION   Anne Mather
WITCHING HOUR   Sara Craven
HILLS OF AMETHYST   Mary Moore
PASSIONATE STRANGER   Flora Kidd
MACLEAN'S WOMAN   Ann Cooper

On sale where you buy paperbacks. If you require further information or have any difficulty obtaining them, write to: Mills & Boon Reader Service, PO Box 236, Thornton Road, Croydon, Surrey CR9 3RU, England.

Mills & Boon
the rose of romance

Mills & Boon
Best Seller Romances

The very best of Mills & Boon Romances

brought back for those of you who missed

them when they were first published.

In August
we bring back the following four
great romantic titles.

STORMY HAVEN
by Rosalind Brett

When Melanie came to the island of Mindoa in the Indian Ocean she was little more than a schoolgirl; when she left, only eight months later, she had grown into a woman. Her scheming cousin Elfrida, Ramon Perez and the masterful Stephen Brent had all played their parts in this transformation.

BOSS MAN FROM OGALLALA
by Janet Dailey

Casey knew she was perfectly capable of running her father's ranch for him while he was in hospital. It was *only* because she was a girl that Flint McCallister had been brought in to do the job. So what with one thing and another, there was hardly a warm welcome waiting for the new boss!

DARK CASTLE
by Anne Mather

What Julie had once felt for Jonas Hunter was now past history and she had made every effort to keep it so. But now she found herself travelling to Scotland to make contact with him again. Could she manage to remain on purely business terms with the man who had meant so much to her and whose attraction for her had increased rather than lessened?

THE GIRL AT DANES' DYKE
by Margaret Rome

'Women aren't welcome at Danes' Dyke,' the inscrutable Thor Halden told Raine; nevertheless circumstances forced him to take her under his roof for a time, and to persuade her to masquerade as his wife. It was a difficult enough situation for Raine, even before she found herself falling in love with him. Would she ever be able to make him trust her?

If you have difficulty in obtaining any of these books through your local paperback retailer, write to:

Mills & Boon Reader Service
P.O. Box 236, Thornton Road, Croydon, Surrey, CR9 3RU.

The Mills & Boon Rose is the Rose of Romance

Every month there are ten new titles to choose from — ten new stories about people falling in love, people you want to read about, people in exciting, far-away places. Choose Mills & Boon. It's your way of relaxing:

August's titles are:

COLLISION by *Margaret Pargeter*
After the heartless way Max Heger had treated her, Selena wanted to be revenged on him. But things didn't work out as she had planned.

DARK REMEMBRANCE by *Daphne Clair*
Could Raina marry Logan Thorne a year after her husband Perry's death, when she knew that Perry would always come first with her?

AN APPLE FROM EVE by *Betty Neels*
Doctor Tane van Diederijk and his fiancée were always cropping up in Euphemia's life. If only she could see the back of both of them?

COPPER LAKE by *Kay Thorpe*
Everything was conspiring to get Toni engaged to Sean. But she was in love with his brother Rafe — who had the worst possible opinion of her!

INVISIBLE WIFE by *Jane Arbor*
Vicente Massimo blamed Tania for his brother's death. So how was it that Tania soon found herself blackmailed into marrying him?

BACHELOR'S WIFE by *Jessica Steele*
Penny's marriage to Nash Devereux had been a ' paper ' one. So why did Nash want a reconciliation just when Penny wanted to marry Trevor?

CASTLE IN SPAIN by *Margaret Rome*
Did Birdie love the lordly Vulcan, Conde de la Conquista de Retz — who wanted to marry her — or did she fear him?

KING OF CULLA by *Sally Wentworth*
After the death of her sister, Marnie wanted to be left alone. But the forceful Ewan McNeill didn't seem to get the message!

ALWAYS THE BOSS by *Victoria Gordon*
The formidable Conan Garth was wrong in every opinion he held of Dinah — but could she ever make him see it?

CONFIRMED BACHELOR by *Roberta Leigh*
Bradley Dexter was everything Robyn disliked. But now that she could give him a well-deserved lesson, fate was playing tricks on her!

If you have difficulty in obtaining any of these books from your local paperback retailer, write to:

Mills & Boon Reader Service
P.O. Box 236, Thornton Road, Croydon, Surrey, CR9 3RU.
Available August 1981